WREATH FOR A LADY

When Mike Torlin takes on the job of investigating the strange happenings at Pete Donati's carnival ground, he figures it's a straightforward case of somebody wanting to put Donati out of business. Then a peculiar chicken is produced out of an egg: a dead girl, shot with slugs from her own shooting gallery. No killer can sidetrack Mike Torlin for long and get away with it — and when the final showdown comes, he is forced to stand his ground and face up to the killer . . .

JOHN GLASBY

WREATH
FOR A LADY

Complete and Unabridged

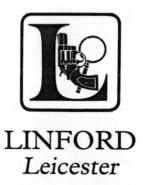

LINFORD
Leicester

First published in Great Britain

First Linford Edition
published 2014

A catalogue record for this book is available
from the British Library.

ISBN 978–1–4448–2048–5

Published by
F. A. Thorpe (Publishing)
Anstey, Leicestershire

Set by Words & Graphics Ltd.
Anstey, Leicestershire
Printed and bound in Great Britain by
T. J. International Ltd., Padstow, Cornwall

This book is printed on acid-free paper

1

Invitation to Murder

At eight forty-five in the morning, Pete Donati's office looked grey and deserted. It was a downtown Chicago district and looked, on the face of it, as though it had seen better days. During the Prohibition days it had been lively enough. There were still a few guys around who could remember it in those days — but not many. I walked up the dingy grey steps, thumbed the bell, and waited. A minute later, the door opened and a tall, thin guy peered down at me over a pair of rimless spectacles.

'Yes?' His voice had a peculiar nasal quality. His age was indeterminate and there was something odd and shifty about the expression in the close-cut eyes that I didn't like.

'I'd like to see Pete Donati,' I said. 'My name's Mike Torlin, private detective.' I handed him my card, then added, 'Donati's been wanting to see me as well.'

A faint flicker of interest showed in the narrowed eyes. He fingered the card helplessly, then gave it back. 'OK, I guess it's all right.' He stood aside and I went into a dusty outer office. The room was completely clear except for a wooden desk and a couple of simple chairs. There was a sheet of cardboard covering a broken pane in the window. I guessed the carnival business must be well into the red, in Chicago at any rate. Then the tall, thin guy came back and said that Mr. Donati was in and would see me right away; would I go through into the other office? I nodded and went inside.

This room was the very opposite of the one I'd just seen. Donati sat behind a huge mahogany desk. The telephone was of white ivory — very expensive. And there was nothing shabby about the way Donati dressed either. I reversed my opinion on the financial status of the carnival business. Donati was wearing a pale grey suit with a dark blood-red tie that stood out vividly against the brilliant whiteness of his silk shirt.

He gave me a brief smile as I came in. 'Won't you sit down, Mr. Torlin.' He gestured towards a comfortable wide-backed chair lined with green plush.

I sat down and waited for him to go on. I couldn't for the life of me see why an important guy like Pete Donati, one of the big names in Chicago show business, should need the help of a private eye. The only guess I had at that moment, was the divorce angle.

He handed me a thick cigar and indicated the silver lighter on the top of the desk near my hand. I lit the cigar and leaned back. 'Perhaps you're wondering why I called you in like this, Mr. Torlin,' he said blandly, lighting a cigar for himself. He leaned back in his chair.

'That's right,' I said.

'I pride myself on being able to guess what's running through your mind this minute,' he went on crisply. 'But I'm afraid it isn't the usual divorce angle, although I don't doubt you've handled plenty of those in your time.'

'It's all part of a private detective's

business,' I said defensively. 'You have to take the rough with the smooth. The rotten breaks with the good.' I detected a touch of veiled mockery in the other's tone and it riled me a little. I grinned at him and tried to look reasonably intelligent, but it was all lost on Donati.

'Just what is it you want me to do?' I asked him. 'I've been hired to do a hell of a lot of strange jobs in my time.' I settled down in my chair.

'This should be quite straightforward, Mr. Torlin.' Donati looked faintly amused. 'I'd like to hire you to find out who's trying to wreck my show. A lot of things have been happening around here during the past few weeks and I refuse to believe that they're all due to coincidence as some people want me to believe.'

'What sort of things, Mr. Donati?' I looked interested.

Donati raised his eyebrows. He wrinkled his nose fastidiously, then went on. 'Two weeks ago, one of the small sideshows was wrecked by a gang of hooligans. I had to write it off as a total loss. Five days ago, some of the rails on the roller coaster were tampered with. Luckily, they were discovered before the show and anybody had been killed. But next time, we may not be so fortunate. That's why I want you to look into the business. Before somebody gets killed.'

I raised my eyebrows. 'You got any ideas who might be behind it? The protection racket, maybe?' I suggested.

'No,' he said morosely. 'I've never had any dealings with such people. There have been no demands for money so far.'

'That checks,' I said. 'I guess we can let them out. Anybody else you know who might want to see you put out of business?'

'Nobody,' he said. His shoulders sagged. 'That's what I'm hiring you to find out.'

'OK,' I said, making up my mind. 'I'll take the job.' I pursed my lips. 'But from where I'm sitting at the moment, things don't look too promising about getting any fast results. Seventy-five dollars a day and expenses.'

He nodded. 'Very well, I'll mail you a cheque this afternoon. And I'll expect results in the very near future.'

I got up. 'I don't guarantee anything,' I said, 'but I'll keep you posted if anything breaks.'

'Fine. Better take a look around during the morning. There's a show on this afternoon, and this evening a special gala performance. Easter Parade and all that. Something special I'm putting on for the others. You'll be able to meet everybody then.'

'Suits me fine,' I said. I went out of the office, through the dusty sepulchre in the front and out into the sunlight. It struck me then that perhaps Donati hadn't been kidding. Maybe there was something more to this game than a bunch of crazy kids, intent on smashing everything up, trying to look big in front of their girlfriends.

I climbed into my Bentley and started her up. If I was getting paid as much as seventy-five dollars a day, it was time I started earning my money. I drove down to the amusement park on the outskirts of Chicago. There were three cars parked at the kerb outside the entrance, but I didn't give them a second thought, and the significance of their presence never hit me until I saw the small crowd gathered around one of the sideshows.

I went over and spotted the thin figure of Lieutenant Hammond in the group. There was a faint buzz of conversation that died immediately as I came up to them.

'Torlin,' said Hammond huskily, and I could hear the click of handcuffs in his voice. 'I might have known you'd be somewhere in on this break. What is it this time?'

'Hello, Charles,' I said quietly. I saw him squirm uncomfortably at the mention of his first name. 'As a matter of fact, this is strictly business as far as I am concerned. I was just hired by Pete Donati to look into some strange happenings that seem to be going on around here.'

Hammond's face hardened. He glared at me. 'Don't call me Charles,' he muttered threateningly.

'OK, Charles,' I said, and watched him go purple in the face. 'What's on your mind?'

Hammond swallowed convulsively. With an effort, he found his voice. 'Since you're in on it, you might as well start with this,' he said. 'But don't get in my hair this time, Torlin, or you'll regret it. Understand?' He stepped aside and I saw, for the first time, the object of their attention. I stood looking down at the crumpled body on the ground for a long moment and I knew that no high-spirited kids from downtown had been responsible for this.

'What the hell?' I asked weakly.

'He must have dropped off the roller coaster,' said Hammond. There was a gleam of satisfaction in his eyes.

I looked up and shaded my eyes against the strong sunlight. I could just make out where the wooden guard rail had been splintered and broken as though by some heavy body falling against it. 'Could it have been an accident?' I looked back to Hammond. My voice sounded as though it had been scraped with gravel.

'If you find the answer to that one, let me know right away,' he said sarcastically.

I ignored that and had another quick

glance at the dead guy. He wasn't pretty and he must have died the minute he hit the ground. The back of his head had been crushed to pulp and there was blood on the gravel. 'Know who he is?' I asked.

Hammond stared at me for a minute, then said: 'His name's Corelli. He was one of the hired hands here. Seems he was working on the roller coaster this morning, checking it on Donati's orders. Whether he fell or was pushed, I've no idea at the moment. There's nobody up there now, that's for sure.'

'Does Donati know?'

'Not yet. I haven't got around to telling him yet. He'll be informed.'

Donati arrived on the scene twenty minutes later. He lit a cigar with fingers that shook a little. I lit a cigarette to keep him company.

'What do you think happened, Torlin?' he said after Hammond finished his spiel. He looked across at me pleadingly.

'Not very much, Donati,' I said. 'But one thing is certain, as I see it. Anybody who hates your guts enough to kill a man like this must be out to finish you for good. There were about a score of characters around here who had the opportunity, and maybe the motive, for killing this guy.'

Hammond rubbed his nose with the back of his hand. 'I'll have the body taken down to the mortuary. As for the rest of you, there are certain questions I want to ask and the answers had better be good. So don't anybody try to leave town until they hear from me.'

I lit another cigarette and thought, to hell with it. Donati had hired me to find out what lay behind all this business at the carnival and my very first morning, I ran into something like this.

Hammond wouldn't ask me too many questions. He would only be wasting time and he knew it. He knew I hadn't been there when the accident had happened and he knew where he could get in touch with me any time he wanted me. He also knew I'd answer his confounded questions, because if I didn't I'd like as not lose my licence and my livelihood; and I wouldn't do that just to shield some crazy maniac who might be around on the loose, killing folk off to even up some old, forgotten score with Pete Donati.

2

The Chicken and the Egg

I got back to the carnival ground at about four in the afternoon. Hammond had brought us down to the local precinct a little before eleven o'clock. It had been one hell of a party, with Hammond doing most of the talking.

The report on the wooden fencing at the edge of the roller coaster hadn't come through by the time Hammond let me go, but I could guess what it would say. Somebody would have sawn through the protecting rails with a fine blade so that it would be unnoticed except on very minute examination. Then when this guy Corelli had leaned back on it, or possibly steadied himself against it, the woodwork had given way, sending him hurtling to his death.

I didn't think there would be any sense in trying to find anybody who had a motive for killing Corelli. He was just unlucky, something incidental to the murder. It could have been anybody. The first guy to go aloft to inspect the roller coaster would get it. If not that day, then tomorrow or the day after.

I found the carnival crowded with people when I arrived. The roller coaster was whizzing along overhead and everybody seemed to be having lots of fun. The fencing, I noticed, had been hastily repaired and the bloodstains cleaned up off the ground. Music was blaring away in the background, a series of strident discords from all sides, pressing on my eardrums. There was a line of sideshows along the edge of the fairground and I decided to start at one end and work my way along. That way, I decided, I wouldn't miss anybody.

The first had a dusty sheet of cloth hanging across the opening at the back. I went inside and bumped into a girl coming along the narrow, dark passage. She was a gorgeous redhead with the milky-white skin and the finely chiselled features that most red-headed girls have.

13

She wore a blue shirt tucked into a pair of light-grey jeans and black, ankle-strap shoes on her feet. There was a red silk scarf knotted loosely around her throat. She stopped suddenly and looked up at me in startled surprise.

'Were you looking for someone?' she asked me.

'Not really,' I told her. 'You'll do for a start, I guess.'

'Just what is it you want?' she asked doubtfully. 'Are you anything to do with the carnival?'

'Again,' I said, 'not really. I've just been hired by Mr. Donati to look into these mysterious happenings on the ground. I believe they've been going on for several weeks now. I just thought this would be as good a time as any to get acquainted with everybody. My name's Torlin — Mike Torlin.'

'A private detective?' She opened her blue eyes a little wider. I wasn't sure whether the surprise on her face was registered or real. Whichever it was, it certainly made her look even more beautiful, and a little more human.

'That's right.'

She led the way into the room behind the small stage of the sideshow. She sat down in a small wooden chair.

'You'll forgive me if we make this interview as brief as possible, Mr. Torlin,' she said to me, 'but I've a job to do in less than a quarter of an hour and I have to get changed.'

'Sure,' I said, grinning. 'Just what do you do around here?'

'That's easy. I'm Helen Crossman. I've worked here with Pete Donati for seven years since I was a kid. I manage the shooting gallery outside.'

'Any idea who might be behind this attempt to break Donati?'

She looked at me disapprovingly. 'None at all. Nobody can have anything against him as far as I know.'

She paused as another thought struck her, then looked up at me sharply. 'Do you think Joe's death might be mixed up in this?'

'Joe?' I asked her.

'Yes. Joe Corelli. Surely you heard about the accident this morning?'

15

'Oh, sure. Yeah. Only I didn't know his name was Joe, and I don't believe it was an accident.'

She moistened her lips with her tongue. 'You think it could be murder then, Mr. Torlin?'

'I'm sure of it,' I said. 'Only it's one thing to be sure and another thing to prove it, particularly to Lieutenant Hammond's satisfaction. He doesn't like private detectives in general, and me in particular.'

'I see.' The smile on her face withered and grew fixed.

'I've got a hunch that what happened this morning was only the beginning,' I said, lighting a cigarette. She shook her head when I offered her the case. 'Maybe something big will break this evening. I gathered from Donati that something special has been laid on for tonight.'

'Yes, that's right. He's got Claire Morgan to come down this evening for the show. Easter Parade and all that, you know.'

Did I detect a trace of bitterness or jealousy in her voice? I wasn't sure so I let it go.

16

'Claire Morgan, the actress?' I said, mildly surprised.

'The same. Pete's organized the highlight of the evening. The Spirit of Easter. Just what it is, nobody seems to know, but one thing about Pete is that he'll spare no expense with these things.'

I nodded. 'Will you be there?'

'I've no idea, Mr. Torlin,' she said tightly. Her eyes seemed to glitter at me. 'I've no idea at all.'

I shrugged my shoulders. 'Oh well, there was no harm in trying.'

'Better luck next time,' she said as I went out of the booth into the fairground again. The harsh glare of the sunlight hit my eyes after the comparative darkness.

By six thirty, I had been round most of the sideshows on the ground. Pete Donati met me under the roller coaster. His face was shining with sweat but he managed to put on a nonchalant front. 'Well, Mike,' he said with a forced heartiness, 'have you met everybody?'

'Just about,' I said.

'Good.' He nodded. 'Know what they all do?'

17

'Most of them, but perhaps you can fill in the details sometime while we're waiting for this show of yours to start. It'll refresh my memory a little. This afternoon has been full of faces and names with few connecting links, and coming so soon after the grilling with Hammond this morning, it's just a little too much.'

Donati nodded. One eyebrow lifted slightly, then he looked up at me. 'You don't seem to be very happy.'

'All my own fault,' I said. 'I always seem to be saying the wrong things to the wrong people all the time.'

'Such as?'

I grinned. 'Helen Crossman for instance. I gathered she didn't like me.'

'Don't worry about Helen,' he said softly. 'That's how she is with everybody at first. She's a nice kid really. Worked here since she was quite small. Her father used to run the shooting gallery for me. Then when he got too old, she just stepped in and took it over. She's made a damned good job of it too.'

'So I noticed.'

I thought about the others I had met

during the afternoon. And I wondered which of them, if any, would have been likely to kill a man just to get rid of Donati.

Sammy Allwood ran the roller coaster: a short, fat guy with eyes that glared out from deep pits in his fleshy features, and a way of moving that suggested a hidden, unsuspected strength in his flabby body. Like an ex-wrestler gone to fat, I decided.

Then there was Josie Kenton, the fortune-teller: forty-ish, hair greying a little but kept at bay with the aid of some kind of dye. She had looked at me as though I had been some rare specimen of animal, just escaped from a museum. Something not to be trusted.

And finally I remembered Sally Benton, Jane Knight and Carmen Phillips, all showgirls of one sort or another: tall, statuesque, natural blondes. I gathered that their main job on the fairground was to act as bait outside the sideshows to lure in the customers. None of them could have been much over twenty-one.

'I suppose all this is going to cost you a packet of dough,' I said after a brief, awkward pause. 'You won't be able to afford many more parties like this one, if these murders continue. Bad for business.'

Donati smiled a little at that. 'With Claire Morgan here tonight, I doubt whether I'll lose much on the deal,' he said. 'She's one of the top-flight actresses back East in New York. She pulls in the crowds wherever she goes. This little act tonight is just a small bit of reciprocal publicity. She gets publicity for her new play opening in Chicago a week tomorrow, and I get the crowds.'

'Sounds fair enough,' I said.

Donati nodded and looked at his watch. 'Time we were getting ready for the show,' he said briskly. 'I want you to see this particularly. It may interest even a private detective.'

'On my salary,' I said, 'anything like this interests me.'

We went into a central tent in the middle of the sideshows. Already, people were streaming in from all directions, being yelled at by the barkers and persuaded to lose their money.

The greatest show on earth, or something like that.

It was cool inside and almost dark. The centre of the tent had been faked up to resemble a vast arena. A single spotlight was swinging aimlessly around as we entered and took our seats. Footsteps sounded on the wooden boards and Sally Benton arrived. She looked better without all the greasepaint on her face, more natural. Quite a good-looker, I decided, then put the thought right out of my mind. Keep your mind on the job in hand, I told myself fiercely. A guy who goes around fooling with the girls while he's hired to investigate a particularly nasty murder case generally loses his job — or sometimes, if he's not too careful, winds up on a slab with the others.

'Hello, Mr. Donati,' she said to Pete. Then she turned her gaze on me and recognized me almost immediately. 'Mr. Torlin,' she said sweetly, 'I thought you were just kidding this afternoon when you said you were a private detective. I thought — ' She broke off helplessly.

I tried to help her. 'That it was just a

21

new line and I was trying to get fresh with you?' I prompted.

'Something like that, I guess.' She bit her lip and turned to Donati. 'When's the big show going to start?'

Donati fidgeted. He seemed oddly ill at ease. 'About twenty minutes from now,' he said, glancing impatiently at his watch. 'I only hope Claire Morgan turns up.'

'You think there's a chance she won't?' I asked sharply.

'No, of course not,' Donati said, but he didn't sound very convincing.

I looked across the arena, then asked, 'What's Claire Morgan like? I've only seen her once. That was back in New York, several years ago. I don't suppose she's changed very much.'

'Not really. She doesn't believe in hiding her light under a bushel. That's why I'm worried she might decide to back out at the last moment.'

I could guess how he was feeling at that instant. Pete Donati was a showman. He had gone to a lot of trouble and expense to put on this show and it had to be good. Not because he stood to lose a couple of thousand dollars if it was a flop, but because he'd lose something far more important as far as he, as a showman, was concerned. He'd lose a lot of personal prestige in the eyes of the people who knew him. I'd already guessed that Donati was a vain character. He had the money to buy a lot of things and he expected people to toe the line.

'By the way,' I asked, turning my head to scan the people sitting around us. 'Anybody seen anything of Helen Crossman?'

'She'll turn up eventually,' said Donati, clearly not interested. 'She's like that. Always arriving late. Thinks it creates an impression. She ought to have been on the stage, I think.'

I looked at my watch. It was nearly seven fifteen. People were shuffling nervously in their seats. A thick, suffocating, clammy silence seemed to have squeezed itself over everything. Here and there was a snatch of muted conversation, but that all died away as the hands of my watch reached seven fifteen, and somewhere in the distance I heard a fanfare of trumpets getting louder.

Pete Donati heaved a sigh of relief and leaned back further in his seat. There was a thunderous tattoo on the drums hidden in the orchestra pit. Then the procession came in. From the beginning it was obvious that Donati hadn't spared any expense with this show. A tremendous Easter Parade.

I couldn't see any sign of Claire Morgan, but right in the centre of the procession, hauled on a decorated float such as one sees in the Mexican carnivals, was a big pink egg tied with a scarlet and gold ribbon. It was about three feet high and at least six feet in length. Slowly, the procession circled the arena, then halted so that the float was directly opposite the place where Donati and I sat.

I could just guess what would happen next: an ingenious method of introducing Claire Morgan. Once again, I appreciated the showmanship of Pete Donati.

All conversation appeared to have died completely. There was a deep waiting silence over everything, as though everybody in the place was holding their breath.

'So that's where she is,' I muttered gently to Donati. 'Inside the egg. Then when it opens, she'll step out of it like Venus rising from the waves.'

He grinned thinly. 'Something like that,' he said softly. 'Perhaps not quite as lurid as you imagine. Nevertheless, I thought it was quite good myself.'

'Then what are you waiting for?' demanded Sally Benton. 'Press the switch that breaks the egg and let's get the party started.'

'All in good time,' said Donati. He got to his feet and lowered himself down into the arena. A moment later he was standing on the float, his face glistening a little with the effort.

'Ladies and gentlemen,' he said loudly, 'tonight, as I promised you, we have Claire Morgan, the talented actress, with us. I hope you'll forgive me the rather spectacular method of introduction. But now, I give you — Claire Morgan.'

He pulled hard at the scarlet and gold

sash. It came away in his hand and the two halves of the egg fell apart. I leaned forward expecting to see Claire Morgan reclining on some golden couch, but there was nothing like that. It wasn't Claire Morgan inside that monster egg, and the girl wasn't reclining. Helen Crossman lay sprawled across a silken cushion, her slender legs twisted beneath her, her eyes wide and staring, glazed and unseeing. There was a circular purple shadow like a bruise between her eyes and a spreading stain of blood on the cushion beneath her head. And resting on her chest, on top of her neatly folded arms, lay a wreath of white lilies.

Donati stood for a long moment, stupefied, staring down at the body. Then he looked appealingly across the arena at me and started to sway slightly. I was in the arena and on to the float in a couple of seconds. Donati was slumped with his head in his hands on the edge of the float. He was making curious animal-like noises deep down in his throat, his fingers twitching and turning in front of his eyes.

Somebody screamed in the audience — a high-pitched feminine voice — and somewhere, the sound of heavy footsteps echoed on the wooden aisles leading up between the rows of seats. Deliberately, I pushed aside the noise and the distracting din into the background of my mind, and looked down at Helen Crossman. That afternoon, in spite of the expression of aloofness on her face, she had been undoubtedly beautiful. But not now. Some women look peaceful in death with everything washed away. Others look indifferent.

But not Helen Crossman. Her lips were drawn back off her teeth in a fierce smile of frozen surprise. The blueness of her eyes contrasted vividly with the pallor of her face. Bending closer, I saw that there was another small hole just behind her left ear. Both shots, I judged, had probably been fired from one of the guns in the fairground shooting gallery.

I felt a little like laughing at the irony of it all. The chicken and the egg. Helen Crossman, alive, had been some chicken. I bit the smile back. Looking down at the pathetic little figure on its red silken couch, it just didn't seem to be funny anymore.

3

Two Ways to Die . . .

Hammond arrived on the scene ten minutes later. The grin faded from his face when he spotted me standing beside the body. 'OK, who is she?' he asked, his voice gritty.

I saw that Donati was in no condition to answer any questions, so I said, 'Her name was Helen Crossman. She ran the shooting gallery out here.'

'You know her?'

'I only met her this afternoon,' I said. 'She didn't strike me as the kind of dame who'd go for a guy, in case you're thinking of the jealousy angle. Something of a manhater if you ask me, although she had the kind of figure a guy would go for.'

'I didn't ask you,' snapped Hammond. He watched until the doctor had made his examination, then asked: 'Well, how did she die, and how long ago?'

29

'Two slugs in the brain fired from close range. You can see the powder burns on the forehead here.' The doc pointed with his forefinger. I shuddered. How guys could look so dispassionately on a dead body, I could never imagine.

'Any idea when she was killed?'

'About three hours ago, I'd say. Maybe two, but certainly not less.'

'And you saw her this afternoon, Torlin.' Hammond whirled on me.

'Sure I did,' I said gently. 'But you can't pin this on me. I left her at about four fifty. She was OK then. Getting ready to go on with the afternoon performance.'

'Four fifty, you say.' Hammond screwed up his mouth. 'Then you might have been the last guy to see her alive.'

'Except one,' I reminded him.

He jerked up his head. 'Who's that?' he snapped.

'The guy who finished her off,' I said pleasantly. 'We mustn't forget about him.'

Hammond straightened up and raised his eyebrows. 'Why should you think that the killer was a man?' he added slowly, shaping every word with his lips. 'A woman could quite easily have pulled the trigger of the gun that killed her.'

'I guess you're right, Lieutenant,' I said promptly. I didn't particularly like the way his questions were leading. It was all very well being hired to find a killer, but to be accused of murder was something very different. I wished I hadn't mentioned knowing Helen Crossman, but Hammond would have found out sooner or later and his suspicious mind would start weaving strange fancies with me as their central character.

There was a thoughtful look in Hammond's eyes. He turned to watch Donati. 'What's the matter with him?'

'I guess he just couldn't stand any more,' I said. 'He was the guy who opened the egg. It was intended to be a surprise. Claire Morgan was supposed to be inside that damned egg. He was standing right next to the body when the egg was opened.'

Hammond nodded again. He looked almost happy, then he pulled himself together. 'This is getting monotonous, Torlin,' he said, and there was that beat of sarcasm in his voice I had detected earlier. 'First this guy Corelli, and now Helen Crossman.'

I took a grip on myself. 'It certainly does look as though we're up against a maniac.'

'Well, Mr. Torlin,' said Hammond eagerly, 'can you think of anybody in particular?'

I shook my head. 'Not at the moment,' I said, 'but if I do, I'll certainly let you know.'

Hammond's face sagged somewhat. 'OK,' he said shortly. 'But don't persist in trying to be the wise guy. You may get your precious licence taken away if you interfere in police affairs. So, I'll warn you again. Keep out of my hair.'

By the time I got outside, it was almost dark. The sun had gone down and the lights were beginning to come out on the roller coaster. I started to walk around the sideshows. Some were deserted, with the guys who ran them still inside the big tent. I wanted to think properly, but with Hammond around, it was impossible.

I looked behind me and saw Hammond

coming out of the entrance to the tent. Behind him came a couple of tall, white-coated guys carrying the pathetic body of Helen Crossman on a stretcher. I felt angry at myself. Somehow, it was as though I was responsible for her being there. She had seemed so full of life and vitality during the afternoon. Now, she lay still and lifeless on a swaying stretcher being carried out of the carnival ground that had been her home ever since she could remember.

I stumbled over a rope looped through a metal pin hammered into the ground, and a split second later something crashed down and thudded into the ground less than two feet from my head. I gave a strangled yelp and pushed myself to my feet, swearing under my breath because my arms were trembling. I could feel the sweat streaming off my forehead. I got close into the base of the rearing structure of the roller coaster and threw a swift glance upwards.

Out of the corner of my eye I caught a glimpse of a dark figure clambering swiftly along the rails. In the darkness, it was impossible to see if it was a man or a woman. Then the figure plunged down into darkness and disappeared. I just stood there, wondering what the hell I was going to do. No sense in climbing up the roller coaster. By the time I struggled to the top it would be deserted and the unknown killer would be well away into the night.

By nature, I'm not a courageous type of guy. I tried my best not to get myself killed, but when somebody started hurling lumps of masonry down at me from the top of the roller coaster, it was time I started to do something — otherwise I wouldn't be around long to do anything about it.

That was the time when heroes should have been made. I walked away from the rising towers of tubular steel and tried not to look back, Nobody seemed to have noticed the incident and it was clear that whoever had tried to murder me had bided their time before dropping that weight on the spot where I would have been had I not fallen over that length of rope.

Stepping out of the darkness of shadow into the lights of the fairground made me feel a little more insecure. I didn't like the idea of an unseen killer trailing me between the sideshows. Especially when I didn't know who it was.

I reached the entrance to the fairground. Hammond was just getting into a police car. He gave me a strange nod and then slammed the door and drove off, the car disappearing into the late-evening traffic with the wail of sirens.

Once inside the Bentley, I started her up and felt the purr of power as I drew away from the kerb. Lighting a cigarette, I tried to concentrate on thinking. Somebody had the idea I knew too much and wanted to see me out of the way, permanently. I tried to think who it might be, then gave it up in disgust.

I needed a drink to settle my nerves. Already, they were screaming at breaking-pitch. The short drive downtown to my office was uneventful. I kept glancing in the rear driving-mirror but nobody seemed to be following me.

Inside the office, I pulled down the

blinds, lit the desk lamp and pulled out my gun from the bottom drawer of the desk. There was a spare clip in another drawer and I slipped it into my jacket pocket. Then I felt a little happier and poured myself a stiff drink. The liquor went down into my stomach and stayed there, exploding in a haze of warmth. I poured another glassful, this time taking the rye further up the glass.

I picked up the phone and dialled Hammond's number. The line buzzed for a minute before he came on the line and grunted. 'Hammond here.'

'This is Mike Torlin,' I said.

'So? What the hell do you want?' His voice was oddly expressionless.

'I just thought I'd let you know there was another attempted murder tonight.'

'What the hell are you talking about? If you're drunk, I'll — '

'I'm not drunk,' I said. 'This is important. Listen if you want to; if not, take the consequences.'

'OK, OK. What have you got to say?' He paused for a moment. 'Who tried to murder who?'

'Somebody tried to brain me with a lump of masonry twenty minutes ago,' I said. 'Don't ask me who it was, because I couldn't see them at the top of the roller coaster.'

There was silence for a moment. 'The roller coaster again,' he said finally. 'Do you want to make a charge?'

'Not particularly,' I said. 'Who can I charge?'

'You have a point there,' he said mildly. 'Come over and make a statement if you want to. It may help with the case.'

'OK,' I said. 'I'll be over in ten minutes.'

I looked at my watch. It was nearly nine o'clock. I poured myself another drink, gulped it down, then went out again.

The Bentley started up as I pressed the starter. I began to pull away from the kerb when another car, without lights, came screeching round the corner, heading straight for me. I caught a glimpse of it as I spun the wheel to get out of the way. Brakes screamed and the car struck the Bentley a glancing blow, turning it over on its side. Glass smashed near my face.

Something stung me across the cheek and I felt the warmth of blood.

Desperately, I fought to open the door. It took all the strength I had to heave it aside and clamber out. For the second time, I stood shaking on the sidewalk and watched the other car vanish around the corner at the end of the street.

I thought that somehow, this game was getting to be a little more dangerous than I had bargained for. Two fool ways in which to die and I had fallen for both of them.

4

Lady in Waiting

The Bentley was in no fit shape to take me anywhere that night. I pushed my way through the small, excited crowd that gathered, quickly conscious of the blood that was oozing down my face from the cut in my cheek.

I was feeling like a physical wreck as I boarded a downtown streetcar and sat down in the back seat. My reflection stared back at me mistily from the glass and I dabbed gingerly at the cut on my face. It wasn't particularly deep but it was stinging like hell.

I got off the streetcar outside the Chicago Homicide Bureau and went inside. The desk sergeant eyed me curiously. He seemed on the point of saying something but I beat him to it.

'OK, I look as though I've been in a fight, so skip the wisecracks. I don't feel in the mood for them at the moment.'

'Careful what you're saying, buster.' He glared at me, and clamped his lips tighter into a hard line across the middle of his granite features. 'Now, what is it that you want?'

'I'd like to see Lieutenant Hammond,' I said sweetly. 'Just tell him that Mike Torlin is here. He'll understand.'

The desk sergeant looked at me with a funny expression in his eyes. It said quite clearly that he didn't think the name Torlin would mean anything to a big guy like Hammond. He hesitated for a moment, then dialled a number on the internal phone. His face changed a bit after that and replacing the phone on its cradle, he jerked a thumb in the direction of a glass-panelled door and said, 'OK, go through there. Hammond's office is the fifth door on the left along the passage.'

I knocked on the door of Hammond's office and walked in. He didn't look too happy to see me. There was a sour expression on his face. 'All right, Torlin, what happened?'

I sat down facing him. 'You know only

40

half of it, Charles,' I said easily.

The veins in his forehead seemed to pop out at that like cords. He opened his mouth like a fish out of water and finally ended up by making a peculiar little gasping sound, halfway between a grunt and a strangled yelp.

'I'll put you in the picture,' I said. 'As I told you over the phone, somebody tried to kill me at the fairground tonight. Whether they thought I was perhaps somebody else or not, I wasn't sure then.'

'But now you are — is that it?' said Hammond sarcastically.

'Right first time, Lieutenant,' I said, 'because they tried it again as I was on my way here.'

'So I see,' muttered Hammond drily. 'If it goes on like this, I might be rid of you after all. Not that I've anything against private dicks personally, but they think they know more than the police. Always coming up with fantastic solutions.'

'Sorry you think that way,' I said.

We sat in silence for several seconds. Then Hammond cleared his throat, looked at me sharply, and said, 'Go on, let's have the full story. Don't spare me any of the more lurid details.'

I grinned and a stab of pain shot through the muscles of my face. 'OK,' I said abruptly. 'Shortly after I left the little party in the tent, somebody dropped half of the Empire State Building from the top of the roller coaster. There was no doubt about it being meant for me. If I hadn't tripped over a guy-rope, it would have brained me.'

'No doubt. Did you see anybody up there?' Hammond rubbed his forehead, easing back the hair from his temples.

I nodded. 'There was somebody up there. They ran along the rails but it was too dark to make out who it was. It could have been a man or a woman.'

'Then what happened?'

'I went straight back to the office and rang you up from there. That was when I said I'd come down here. The murderer made another try just as I got into my car. Another sedan without lights came round the corner on two wheels and smashed into me. That's where I got this.' I fingered the cut on my cheek.

We sat in silence again for a while.

'Obviously somebody thinks you know too much,' went on Hammond quietly, drumming with his fingers on the top of the desk. 'So it must be somebody you met yesterday afternoon'

'That's a point,' I said thoughtfully. 'I'll bear it in mind.'

'You mean you're still going through with the case?'

'That's what I'm being paid for.'

Hammond spread his hands wide. 'It's your neck I suppose,' he said. He straightened up in his chair. 'Just how much do you know about this case? The truth now.'

'Not much,' I told him. 'I'm probably as much in the dark about the affair as you are. Pete Donati hired me yesterday morning to discover why somebody seems to be trying to put him out of business by faking accidents all over the carnival. Now it seems to have culminated in a double murder.'

I lit a cigarette and tried to forget the twisted face of Helen Crossman, lying in her own blood on a couch of red silk, a wreath of white lilies on her breast.

A wreath for a lady.

'How much do you guys know?' I asked Hammond. 'Maybe we could help each other on this case.'

'Yeah, maybe.' He seemed to be thinking that one over. 'But who gets the news first if anything important breaks? Me or your client?'

'Why you, of course, Lieutenant,' I said promptly.

'Well. So long as you stick by that.'

He moved some papers to one side and came up with a photograph, which he pushed across the desk towards me.

'Know who this is, Torlin?'

I picked up the photograph and studied it, but I didn't need a second glance to tell me who it was.

'Pete Donati,' I said, surprised.

'Right first time,' grinned Hammond. 'Now take a close look at this.'

He handed me another photograph, this time of a guy in a prison outfit. The likeness was there but it wasn't very pronounced. There were certain surface changes, although the structural details of both faces were very alike.

'Donati's twin brother,' I suggested.

'Try again.'

'Not Donati, surely?'

Hammond nodded. 'That's right. We located the guy who altered his face for him. That was way back in the early thirties, but he certainly made a damned good job of it.'

'Then what's his real name?' I asked. The guy in the prison garb looked oddly familiar, but I couldn't place him.

'Johnny Leinster.' Hammond nodded as he saw the expression of surprise on my face. 'Yeah, that's the guy. One of the biggest hoodlums of the thirties.'

'But I always thought he'd been killed during the battles.'

Hammond shook his head. 'Not on your life. Johnny Leinster just dropped out of the public eye for a couple of years until everything had blown over. Then he got hold of this plastic surgeon to fix him up with a completely new face, came out here, bought a carnival, got mixed up with the high society of Chicago, and launched himself as Pete Donati, the big showman.'

I whistled. Little things began to slip into place, to add up and make sense. Johnny Leinster and Pete Donati, the same guy. It meant that any of his old-time associates might still be harbouring a grudge against him. A big-time hoodlum makes a lot of enemies. A hell of a lot. But it also meant that I was virtually back where I had started, because it let in so many suspects that you had to take in nearly the whole of the population to be sure of getting the right guy.

'So that's where all the big hoodlums go when the going gets a little too tough for them.' I stubbed out my cigarette in the tray. 'A pity I didn't know this before I agreed to take the job.'

Pete Donati the showman, alias Johnny Leinster, Big Man of the Chicago underworld. It made a funny kind of sense.

'As for the murder of Helen Crossman,' went on Hammond, as though I hadn't spoken, 'we know she was killed at about five o'clock in the afternoon. You say you were with her at four-fifty, so she was killed almost immediately after you left her.'

'We found the gun that did it — no fingerprints, but we didn't expect to be that lucky — and the doc says she was shot from a distance of less than a foot. In fact, it's probable that the gun was right up to her forehead when the murderer pulled the trigger.'

'How about the guy who fell from the roller coaster during the morning?'

Hammond shrugged. 'He's still down in the mortuary somewhere. We've already decided that his death has no real significance. It could have been anybody. I've got a couple of men checking on the saw that was used to cut through the protecting rail.'

'Any marks on Helen Crossman's body?'

'No — why?'

'Well, it just seems funny that anybody should sit quite still while somebody puts a gun to their forehead and quietly pulls the trigger. You can't fire one of those fairground rifles with one hand and hold a struggling dame with the other.'

Hammond wrinkled his forehead. 'That's a point I'd overlooked,' he said slowly.

'Thanks for mentioning it.'

'It was nothing,' I said, getting up. 'I'll let you know if anybody else takes a pot shot at me.'

'Do that,' said Hammond. He turned back to the reports on his desk. It didn't look as though he was going to get much sleep that night. I was glad I was a private detective. At least I could generally sleep when I felt like it.

I walked back to my office, hoping to put my feet up on the desk for a while before turning in. I had a lot of things to think out. Important things. But I didn't have any chance to put my feet up because when I pushed open the door of my office, I saw I had a visitor.

'I've been waiting nearly an hour to see you, Mr. Torlin,' said Sally Benton. 'I was just on the point of leaving. I hope you don't mind me coming in here like this.'

'Not at all,' I said. 'To tell the truth, I'd rather have you here than some of the people who've been in this office in the past.'

She flushed a little at that and looked down at her shoes.

'What can I do for you?' I asked her.

I shut the door and she sat down a little uncomfortably in the chair beside the desk, the one I reserved for special clients. She seemed ill at ease, as though she had some deep problem on her mind. Maybe she had been drinking after seeing Helen Crossman's body come to light in that great pink egg. Her eyes were a little vacant, but she seemed all right. I handed her a glass of bourbon and she sipped it slowly, grimacing a little. I guessed she wasn't a heavy drinker, and that made me feel better somehow.

I sat down and put my feet up on the desk. 'What's the trouble?' I asked.

'After I got home this evening, I got to thinking about Helen. The way she looked inside that, that — ' She shuddered and screwed up her eyes for a moment, then took a quick, deep gulp of the bourbon. Squaring her shoulders, she looked me in the eye and went on. 'I remembered how you were associated with this case and I thought you'd be the right man to contact.'

I nodded. 'If you've anything on your

mind, you can tell me,' I said. 'I'm as determined to get to the bottom of this mess as you are. Maybe more so, since somebody seems to be taking a very personal interest in my welfare.'

She looked a little surprised at that. 'You mean somebody tried to kill you, Mr. Torlin?'

'That's right,' I answered, 'but let's hear your problem. What's troubling you, honey?'

If she didn't go for the 'honey' routine she gave no outward sign. Instead, she said quietly, 'There are some things I thought you ought to know about Helen Crossman.'

'Go ahead,' I said. 'I'm listening. Let's have your version of it.'

'I don't pretend to know who killed Helen, but she wasn't the shy, retiring type a lot of people seemed to think she was.'

'You mean she went around with some steady guy?'

Sally Benton nodded. 'I don't know who he was, but I saw him several times going into the back entrance of the shooting gallery where she worked. Once

I saw them together in the city in one of the nightspots.'

'Did they act as though they were friends?' I wanted to know.

'I think so.'

'What kind of an answer is that?'

'Well . . . ' She twisted her fingers together. 'Yes, they seemed to be on very good terms with each other.'

I ground out the stub of my cigarette slowly. 'I see. Would you recognize this guy again if you saw him?'

'Oh yes.'

'You're sure?'

'I'm positive.'

'Good. Then let me know if you ever see him again. It may give us an important lead. And thanks for telling me all this. Things are beginning to add up, but only slowly. I haven't really seen the light yet.'

Sally Benton got to her feet. 'Glad I was able to help, Mike,' she said, and there was a warm, hungry look in her eyes. 'Will you be around tomorrow?'

'It's tomorrow already,' I said, glancing down at my watch.

'You know what I mean.'

'Sure,' I said. 'I'll be around somewhere.'

'I'll maybe hold you to that, Mike.' Her voice was gentle and husky. She came a couple of steps closer. 'I hope you're on this case for a long time, Mr. Torlin,' she said, and shot me a meaningful glance.

I watched her walk with dignity and a faint sway down the steps and into the street. As I watched her go, I thought that either Sally Benton was a damned good liar, or she really had meant what she had said. I hoped it was the latter.

I kept on thinking. There were plenty of leads in this case, but it was more than likely that most of them would lead me up a blind alley. There was one person, however, who might make a worthwhile contribution to the general fund of knowledge. The one person who hadn't turned up when she should. Funny how everybody seemed to have forgotten her for some reason or other.

Claire Morgan.

The woman that Helen Crossman had deputised for with such a spectacular, and final, result.

5

Death of an Actress

The next morning, I went uptown to try and locate Claire Morgan. The Bentley had been fixed for me by an all-night garage and was just about as good as new. On the way, I smoked a cigarette and tried to figure out where Claire Morgan fitted into this deal. She'd been booked to turn up on that float in Pete Donati's Easter Parade; only, a very dead Helen Crossman had turned up instead. So even to a stupid guy like me, that looked as though Claire Morgan had either been tipped off about the murder or, at least, knew something about it.

Whatever the reasons for her not turning up for the party as advertised the previous night, I figured I ought to know something about it. The theatre where Claire Morgan was playing the lead was a lush place near the middle of the city.

Outside, in big lights, I could see her name spelled out above the imposing entrance. Some dame, I decided: one who'd reached the top of her particular tree and intended to stay there no matter what went on below.

I checked my watch. Nearly nine o'clock. It was possible they were already at rehearsals. If so, I'd have one hell of a job getting an interview with her, particularly if I was right and she knew as much as I thought she did. I parked the Bentley near the side entrance and waited while I finished my cigarette. A couple of well-dressed dames went inside but nobody came out. I figured that if I went barging in, there'd be a bouncer with plenty of muscles on the other side of that door, itching to throw me out on the sidewalk on my neck, pointedly ignoring the five-dollar bill in my hand.

Finally, I made up my mind. I stepped out of the Bentley, ground the stub of the cigarette beneath my heel on the sidewalk, and made my way towards the side entrance. Inside the theatre, I seemed to be completely on my own. A thin-faced guy inside a small office poked his head out and said thinly:

'Looking for somebody special, mister?'

'Yeah.' I nodded. There wasn't any point in pussyfooting it around the place. I'd get nowhere fast like that. 'Can you tell me where I can find Miss Morgan?'

'You're aiming rather high, aren't you, mister?' He had a thin, whining voice that grated on my nerves. His eyes were small and mean and his jaw stuck out. He began to move out of his cubbyhole and came round towards me.

I said to him: 'Just you mind your business, friend, and I'll do the same. Now — where can I find Claire Morgan?'

'You a friend of hers?'

'In a way.' I guessed it was time I stopped this two-way argument so I took out my official business card and flashed it at him. There was a five-dollar bill inside.

He nodded at that and his eyes grew even meaner. Then he licked his lips, nodded, and took the bill. 'Now you're talking my kind of language. Why didn't you say that before?'

He slipped the bill into his pocket and jerked a thumb in the direction of the end of the dark passage.

'Along there, but I doubt whether you'll be able to see her just now. They're rehearsing for the new play at the moment. Maybe I could get you a seat out front.' He twitched his fingers together.

'That'd suit me just fine,' I said. He took the ten-spot, gave it a brief, appreciative glance, then slipped it in beside the other bill.

Inside the theatre, it was cool and dark, the only light coming through a wide window in the high roof and a spotlight swinging lazily around the stage. I slipped into the seat on the end of the front row and kept as quiet as I could. Four other guys were sitting in the centre of the row, two in shirtsleeves with scripts on their knees and cups of coffee at their elbows. The others looked like the backers of the play. It wasn't until I looked at them more closely that I realized one of the guys in the slick suits was Johnny Leinster.

Somehow, I'd got out of the way of

thinking of him as Pete Donati — the name just didn't seem to fit him. So he was one of the backers of the show. Didn't think he'd come all the way to the theatre just for the ride. He must have had a packet of dough sunk in this business.

He saw me instantly and there was a strange glitter in his eyes. Then he waved a hand negligently and turned back to the guy on his right. All four of them looked slightly bored with the proceedings. I couldn't follow the action of the play too well. It was way above my head and the frequent interruptions from the guys in the shirtsleeves out front made it even more difficult.

Claire Morgan had the leading role, as expected: a somewhat free-living wife who was eventually shot by a jealous husband in the last act. Watching it, I began to feel bored also, and wondered if the fifteen bucks I'd given the doorman hadn't been a dead loss. Still, I could always put it on the expense account. Johnny Leinster looked as though he could afford it.

Towards the end of the final act, I felt like getting up and walking out. Claire Morgan was a magnificent actress, but even she couldn't possibly hope to pull the rest of a ham cast along with her and try to give life to a corny plot at the same time. I figured the guys who paid the prices they were asking for the tickets to see this ham acting were either mad or loaded with too much dough.

How I sat through that rehearsal I shall never know. Claire Morgan stood in the centre of the stage with the spotlight on her, ready for the final dramatic act. I knew she'd play it like a veteran. Finally discovered in her double-dealing, she stood awaiting the arrival of her outraged husband. The spotlight swung to the door a split second before it burst open. It was ham acting all the way. The guy rushed in almost foaming at the mouth, the gun in his hand. He stood there for a moment, swaying on his feet; then, with a hoarse laugh, he lifted the gun and pulled the trigger.

The least that could be said for the play was that the sound effects were most realistic. Claire Morgan clutched at her breast and the red stain of scarlet ink came filtering between her fingers. Her face took on a vacant expression and seemed to twist as she fought to get the words out. Then her whole body convulsed as a spasm shook her. For an instant, she remained upright, fumbling for the table behind her but not finding it. Then she went down on her face in as good a death scene as I'd ever witnessed. The curtain fell to a sudden thunderous roll from the solitary drummer in the orchestra pit.

Out of the corner of my eye, I saw Johnny Leinster coming towards me. He crushed into the seat beside me and said in a husky voice:

'Didn't expect to see you here today, Mike. Looking for something?' He slewed round in his seat and took a close look at me.

'Just trying to get results,' I said. 'You know me, Mr. Donati. It struck me last night that Claire Morgan should know more about this business than is good for her. She never turned up at your party last night, which to me means that she was probably tipped off about the murder. Anyway, I'd like to ask her a few questions, if you've no objection.'

'None at all, Mike,' he said affably. But I thought I could detect a note of puzzled bewilderment in his voice. And I could see that he wasn't quite himself this morning.

'I'm just trying to justify my existence,' I said quietly. There was a lot of movement going on behind the curtain, but I couldn't see what was happening. 'It's time you got some results for your money.'

'You're too modest,' he said. 'I'm quite satisfied. I don't have any worries in that direction, though I doubt whether Claire can tell you anything you don't already know.'

I sucked in my cheeks. 'You can never tell,' I told him. 'I'm learning quite a lot this morning. Maybe this is going to be my lucky day. I never knew you were interested in this play.'

He shrugged. 'If I think it's good, I'll back it. The society in this city go for

60

anything they can't understand. If they can't figure it out for themselves, the critics will call it high art and give it rave notices.' He nodded to the big guy in the monkey suit sitting in front of the stage, who eased himself out of his seat and went out of one of the exit doors.

I thought it was about time I put some of my cards on the table. 'I also learned something interesting last night from Lieutenant Hammond,' I said slowly, watching him carefully. 'It concerns a guy called Johnny Leinster.'

He swung round on me at that, his features twisted. His face darkened. Then he pulled himself together and said weakly: 'Johnny Leinster.' He grinned. 'What about him?'

'Don't you think it's about time you were frank with me, Donati?' I said harshly. My fingers were sticky and the sweat had popped out on the palms of my hands. 'You're Johnny Leinster. It's no concern of mine, but if you'd told me that in the first place I might have had something to go on.'

'Why you dirty, double-crossing — '

'Steady, Johnny,' I said sharply, without raising my voice. 'Nobody knows anything about this but the Lieutenant and myself. As far as I'm concerned, you're going straight; and so long as I get my money regularly, I'll consider myself hired to find the killer for you. But I need straight answers to a lot of important questions.'

His shoulders sagged a little. 'OK, Mike. You win, I guess. Any other time, you wouldn't stay alive long after finding out anything like this; but if Hammond knows it as well — and I'll have to take your word for that — I don't suppose there's any sense in reverting back to the old ways and taking you for a ride.'

'I'm glad you see it that way, Johnny,' I said. 'Believe me, it's the best for both of us.'

'Maybe.' He broke off as one of the guys in the play came rushing over and whispered something in his ear.

Johnny looked round at me slowly. 'I guess it was a good thing you were around, Mike,' he said. His voice was gentle, but shocked. 'I think you'd better come with us. Claire Morgan wasn't acting just now. That gun they used was really loaded.'

I got slowly to my feet, feeling sick. 'No,' I said from between my teeth. 'Not another one of them.'

Leinster looked shaken in spite of his calm exterior. There was an unearthly pallor on his face. Maybe he was thinking about the bad publicity if this news got around to the newspapers and somebody at Police Headquarters started probing into his past. Maybe that way, Johnny Leinster would come back into the public eye sooner than was anticipated. Or perhaps he was visualizing the thousands of dollars he stood to lose without Claire Morgan in the leading role in the play; maybe without any play at all.

We went out of the auditorium, Indian file: Leinster first, the tall guy still in his stage clothes close up behind him, and then me. We climbed up onto the stage and pushed through the heavy curtain.

There was a guy bending over the still body of Claire Morgan and I recognized him as the outraged husband who had pulled the trigger. He wasn't looking so outraged now.

I took a quick look at Claire Morgan. No doubt about it. She was dead, very dead. There hadn't been anything wrong with that guy's aim, in spite of his ham acting. I saw that the bullet had gone in just above the heart, killing her instantly.

I straightened. Leinster was watching me curiously.

'Better get in touch with Hammond,' I said to him. 'I can just imagine what he'll say about this.'

6

Who Said Blackmail?

With Claire Morgan dead, there was no point in asking her any questions. The guy who'd pulled the trigger knew nothing about it, of course. He'd picked up the gun from the props man, expecting it to be full of blanks. He was shaking like a leaf by the time the fact penetrated his artistic brain that a murder had been committed. When I told him Lieutenant Hammond of Homicide was on his way over, he almost passed out at my feet.

'I swear I had nothing to do with it,' he said pleadingly. 'I didn't know there were live slugs in that gun. If I had, I'd never have used it.'

'Sure, I believe you,' I told him in a crisp, business-like voice. 'You've nothing to worry about. If you put those slugs in that gun yourself, you wouldn't be such a fool as to use it yourself.'

'You think the Lieutenant will see it that way?'

'Sure thing,' I said innocently.

At that moment Hammond arrived, followed by a retinue of photographers, the police doctor, and a couple of other guys I didn't recognize — but from the way they walked across the stage, I guessed they hadn't been off the beat for very long.

'Damn it, Torlin,' he exploded as he parted the curtains and climbed up onto the stage, 'I thought I warned you about getting into my hair. What the hell are you doing here?'

I grinned. 'I told you I'd let you know if anything happened, Charles,' I said. 'Well, it has. Can I help it if I seem to attract murder?'

Hammond swore under his breath, then bent to examine the body. He took a deep breath as he straightened up.

'Where's the gun?' he asked pointedly.

Leinster brought it over to him. Hammond sniffed it expertly, flicked open the chambers, then nodded.

'OK.' He handed it to one of the other guys. 'Get it checked for fingerprints.' He glared around the assembled company. 'Let's have it. Anybody know how a live slug might have got into that gun?'

If he was expecting a confession, he was disappointed. Nobody spoke. Finally, he turned to Leinster. 'Just what were your relations with Claire Morgan?'

The other shrugged. 'We were just business friends, that's all. I knew her from way back. When she told me she wanted to star in a play in Chicago, I thought I'd back the show for old times' sake.'

'That all there was to it?'

'That's all, Lieutenant.'

I could see by Leinster's face that it wasn't all there was to it, but I didn't say anything. After all, he was my client, even though he had been a big shot in the early Chicago rackets. And his cheque of the previous day had been good, so I had nothing to worry about. There was no sense in killing the bird that laid the golden eggs. Not while he kept on paying. After all, a guy had to eat.

The way the case was turning out, I doubted whether I could get another client who'd live long enough to pay me.

'I'll question everybody one at a time.' Hammond turned abruptly. 'You two guys,' he said, 'see that nobody leaves the building until I give the OK.'

'Sure, Lieutenant,' one of them said. I watched them climb off the stage, split up at the bottom and take both entrances to the theatre.

The questioning lasted all morning and the routine was much the same as it had been when Joe Corelli had dropped to his death off the roller coaster. Only this time, Hammond knew it was murder and he didn't mean to let anything slip through his fingers if he could help it.

At the end of it all, he drew a complete blank. As I thought he would. Any murderer who intended to kill his victim in full view of an audience, as Claire Morgan had been killed, wouldn't leave much behind in the way of clues. I was also willing to stake my licence and my reputation that he'd find nothing on the gun but the prints of the guy who'd pulled the trigger, and maybe the prop man.

'OK,' he said finally. 'You can all go. But don't try to leave town. I may want you all for further questioning. That goes for you, too, Torlin.' He gave me a nasty look.

'Now what did I do, Lieutenant?'

'Nothing so far, except get under my feet. Hell, you stick to me closer than my shadow.'

He stormed out of the theatre and five minutes later, the meat wagon arrived to take away the dead body of Claire Morgan. At least, I thought, slipping behind the wheel of the Bentley, she'd died as she had lived, on the stage. But it seemed such a crummy way to die — and for no reason that I could see, unless it was to prevent her from talking to me. I thought about that and decided it was as good a reason as any for wanting Claire Morgan out of the way.

I chain-smoked steadily on the way back to the office and thought some more. There was a lead to the identity of the killer somewhere in this maze of murders and faked accidents if I could only see it — somewhere just under my nose. I thought how Claire Morgan had been killed. Then there had been Helen Crossman — both women shot. And each time, Leinster, or whoever he cared to call himself, had been somewhere in the vicinity.

Nobody would think of asking any awkward questions if the boss asked to examine the gun that was to be used in the rehearsal. He could quite easily have put in that live cartridge, knowing full well that Claire Morgan would get it in the heart. But what was his motive? I couldn't see any guy killing off his leading lady for nothing, especially if it meant the headache of losing a few thousand bucks. Had Leinster got the sense of humour that seemed to be associated with each of these killings? There had been something diabolically funny about them all, something really subtle. I nodded my head. They all had one thing in common: showmanship. It fitted Leinster like a glove, I decided.

I threw the stub of my cigarette out of

the window of the car and thought some more. It would have to be an overpowering hate for a guy to do anything like that against himself. First, wrecking his own carnival with a series of senseless accidents culminating in murder. Secondly, killing his big act in full view of an audience of several hundred. And now, throwing more bucks down the drain by murdering Claire Morgan. It just didn't make sense. I began to wish I'd taken on something easy like joining the Foreign Legion.

I could have gone on thinking like that for a long while, only I reached the office and the phone was already ringing shrilly. I picked it up, expecting to hear Sally Benton's voice; only it was Hammond's, and the thrill sagged.

'Yes?'

'That you, Torlin?'

'Who else did you expect?' I asked.

'OK. Cut out the funny business. I just thought I'd let you know that I've pulled in your favourite client, Donati, on a charge of murder.'

'You're joking, Hammond,' I said.

He chuckled drily. 'I thought you'd take it that way. But get down to the Bureau if you want to see him for anything important.'

'You're damned right I will,' I said and slammed down the phone.

The Bentley was working overtime. Within ten minutes I was at the Homicide Bureau. The desk sergeant recognized me instantly as I entered and nodded to me to go right inside.

Hammond was alone in his office. He looked up sharply as I walked in, then grinned triumphantly. 'Sit down, Torlin,' he said affably. 'I want to have a little talk with you.'

'Go ahead,' I retorted. 'The desire's mutual.'

His grin widened. 'I realize Leinster's your client, Torlin, but these things happen. Maybe you can find some other guy after we send him to the electric chair.'

'Get to the point,' I said impatiently. I had the feeling I was being made to look a fool and I didn't like it.

'We aren't altogether fools, you know,'

began Hammond with a forced politeness, 'even though some people seem to think so. For instance, did you know that Leinster was being blackmailed?'

He shot the question at me sharply and leaned forward, watching me like a hawk.

I looked suitably surprised and impressed. 'No, I didn't. But I'll take your word for it.'

'Any idea who it was?'

I shook my head. 'None at all. But I can guess he made a packet of enemies in the old days.'

'True enough.' Hammond nodded and pulled his nose between the thumb and forefinger of his right hand. 'Only they do say that hell holds no fury as a woman scorned.'

I lit a cigarette and leaned back in my chair. 'Go on.'

'We've got enough evidence on your client to send him to the chair a dozen times. Claire Morgan had been blackmailing him for the past twenty years or so. Maybe that'll surprise you.'

I kept my hands on my knees and stared at him. Then I said harshly: 'And

73

you think that's why he killed her? To keep her quiet and put an end to her blackmailing?'

'It looks that way to us.' His smile broadened still further. 'Don't take it too hard, Torlin. We all make mistakes at one time or another. You made one when you accepted Leinster as your client. There were two things you didn't know then: that he was Johnny Leinster, and that he was being blackmailed by one of his old associates.'

I sat up straight at that last remark. 'Claire Morgan, an associate of Johnny Leinster's?'

'Of course.' He shook his head pityingly. 'We started digging back into her past this morning. It wasn't all savoury, you know. Oh sure, she'd been one of the top-flight actresses back east for several years. But in the twenties and thirties it was different.'

I felt defeated. What does a guy do when he gets that thrown at him? I said, 'Can I see my client?'

'Sure.' Hammond got up and led the way out of the room. At the end of the passage, we found Leinster in one of the cells. At least he had the place to himself. Hammond produced a bunch of keys and opened the door. I went inside and heard it clang behind me with a hollow din, and the sound sent funny little shivers running along my spine.

Wearily, I sat down next to Leinster. For once, he didn't look too pleased with himself. Some of his old confidence seemed to have evaporated during the morning and early afternoon.

Hammond went away, leaving us both together.

7

Under Suspicion

Leinster gave me a crooked grin. He shifted uncomfortably in his chair. 'Glad you were able to come down, Mike,' he said with a forced quietness — but there was the look of a hunted animal about him that I noticed right away. 'There are a lot of things I guess I ought to tell you.'

'Fire away, Johnny,' I said. I'd got used to thinking of him as Johnny Leinster, the ex-mobster, now. The name Pete Donati didn't seem to mean anything. 'Hammond been giving you the works?'

'Sure, he gave me a rough time. He's sure I killed Helen and Claire.'

'And did you?' I asked sharply.

'Damn you, Torlin. Whose side are you supposed to be on in this case?'

'OK, OK. Sorry Johnny, but I've got to know the answer to that particular question if I'm to go on any further.'

He sank back wearily. 'Got a cigarette? They took mine away.'

'Sure.' I handed him the packet and he took one. I lit it for him and then took one for myself. He inhaled noisily and blew out a cloud of smoke. I noticed his fingers were trembling slightly on his knees.

'I didn't kill either of them, Torlin. And you know it.'

'Fair enough,' I said. 'That takes care of question number one. Now — have you got any idea who might have wanted them dead?'

He shook his head. 'That's the frightening part about it all. I can't think of anybody.'

'Then we'll just have to start from scratch,' I told him. 'What about your lawyer? Phoned him yet?'

'Yeah.' Leinster nodded. 'He's on his way over here now.'

'Then what are you worrying about? A smart lawyer will get you off the hook in no time at all. Hammond may bluster about it, but I know him. I'm only a private detective but I do know that it doesn't matter what he thinks he knows, it's evidence that counts, and he's got to produce that — together with a motive.'

'Do you think I haven't thought about that? He's got evidence. All he wants is to send me to the chair. And he's got motives, too.' Leinster spoke in a low voice. I could see he was scared. Sweat had popped out on his forehead. Ever seen a rat running around in a box?

'Come to think of it, Hammond did mention something about blackmail a couple of minutes ago. Was he just bluffing, or does he really have something?'

Leinster hesitated and I saw the scared glance in his eyes. His whole body seemed to sag.

'Better tell me everything,' I suggested gently. 'It's bound to come out in the end and the sooner I know about it and what's behind it all, the better my chance of finding out who did kill Helen Crossman and Claire Morgan.'

'I guess you're right, Torlin.' He sounded like a guy who'd just met with final and utter defeat. A one-time big shot who'd gone straight to escape a shady past and now faced the prospect of going to the 'Big Burn' for something he hadn't done.

He moistened his lips. He thought deeply for a moment and I let him take his time.

'Since you're working for me, your relationship is the same as that of a lawyer — right?' he asked.

I nodded in agreement. 'If you're thinking about me talking — especially to the cops — don't,' I said. 'This is absolutely confidential.'

He seemed more at ease at that. 'It's true what Hammond says. How he got hold of it, I don't know. Claire Morgan was blackmailing me. She had been for years.'

'But why? What possible hold could she have over you?'

'Isn't that easy to guess?' he muttered bitterly.

'I suppose it is,' I said weakly. 'She knew who you were. Johnny Leinster, Chicago big shot, is that it?'

'That's most of it,' he agreed finally.

'Was there any more?'

'She had a bunch of clippings from the newspapers of those days.'

'About you and the rackets?'

'That's right.'

'I see.' I was beginning to get a little worried now. It was beginning to look as though even a smart lawyer wouldn't stand a snowball in hell's chance of springing Johnny Leinster of this rap. I could see now why Hammond had seemed so triumphant. He had most of the jokers from the pack in his own hand.

'But why should she want to blackmail you? Seems to me you were on pretty good terms with her.'

'Don't let that fool you,' he said bitterly. 'She hated my guts, deep down. I guess it all started a long way back. Remember the time of Prohibition?'

I nodded.

'She was Mayor Henson's daughter. High society standing and all that. But we got together. I had the dough she craved and she possessed the breeding. Maybe we thought a bit of each would rub off on to the other, I don't know. Does anybody know why we did those crazy things in the roaring twenties and thirties?'

'Not really, I suppose,' I agreed.

'Towards the end I had to get out. You can see how it was.'

'Sure,' I said impatiently. 'Don't bother to go into details. I'm beginning to get the general picture.' I stood up. There were more footsteps coming along the passage and I picked out Hammond's voice.

'Sounds as though your lawyer finally got here,' I said. 'The best of luck. I'll let you know if anything breaks in the near future.'

'Thanks,' he replied drily. He nodded his head, then got up and came right up to me. 'Before you go I think you ought to know something. Maybe it's important, maybe not.'

'Spill it,' I said softly.

'Keep your eyes open for a guy called Moose Madison. It's just possible he's back in town. You can easily check on this and if it's true, he may have something to do with these killings.'

'Moose Madison?' I looked puzzled.

'That's right.' His voice was just a

whisper. 'He was with me back in the old days. He went to 'Big Q' for twenty years for his part in the National Bank robbery. Maybe he still thinks I owe him something.'

'Have you heard from him lately? Any threatening notes, demands for money?' I asked quickly. A key was grating metallically in the lock at my back.

He shook his head swiftly.

'OK,' I said loudly. 'Thanks for the information, Mr. Donati. It's given me something to go on. I'll let you know how things pan out.'

I had a good look at his lawyer as I left the cell. He was a tall, polished guy with black hair slicked back from his forehead, brushed so that it shone. There seemed to be a permanent sneer fixed on his features and his smile was a little too artificial to register with me.

Clive Rookman. One of the smoothest mouthpieces in the business. I could guess why Leinster had hired him to handle the case. But personally I wouldn't have trusted him as far as I could throw him with one hand tied behind my back.

Hammond closed the cell door behind me and followed me along the passage, his jaw set. 'Get anything out of him you think I ought to know?' he asked finally.

'Such as what?' I asked him. 'Were you expecting a confession?'

'Don't try to be funny, Torlin,' he grated. 'Remember, I can bust you any time I feel like it.'

'I'll remember,' I promised.

Two fifteen in the afternoon. I'd got one break but I'd also lined up a score of questions to which I didn't know the answers. Perhaps if I could locate this guy, Moose Madison, it might help. But I didn't even know where to start looking, and Chicago is a big enough place when it comes to trying to find one particular guy.

I decided to take a look around Claire Morgan's dressing room. If I could lay my hands on those old newspaper clippings before Hammond did, I'd be able to break down one of the strongest links in Hammond's chain of evidence.

There was a different guy just inside

the side entrance of the theatre when I got there. He glared down resentfully at me from a height of a little over six-feet-four. He had the shoulders to match. 'I'm afraid you can't come in here,' he said hollowly. 'The police have closed the place until further notice.'

'That's OK.' My laugh ended on the fourth 'ha' as I saw that it wasn't OK. I took out my card. 'I'm working on this particular case,' I said. 'Donati's my client.'

He eyed the card thoughtfully, then handed it back to me. 'I've got orders from Lieutenant Hammond to keep the place closed to everybody,' he persisted sullenly. 'I don't want to lose my job over this.'

'Would thirty dollars see you all right?'

The mean look came back into his eyes. He held out his hand and took the sheaf of bills. 'OK, mister. But make it snappy before Hammond gets back. Here's a key.'

Claire Morgan's room was easily recognized by the great silver star over the door. I opened it with the key the bruiser had given me, slipped inside, and locked the door behind me. No sense in taking stupid chances, I decided.

The room was bigger than I had expected, with a smaller room leading off the main one. There was a big vase of flowers — red carnations — in front of the mirror, and the whole place looked expensive. There was a small envelope attached to the carnations and a card inside. It was signed simply 'M'. Not Johnny Leinster.

Madison?

It was a thought.

I went through the drawers but there was nothing in them of importance. A pile of newspaper cuttings all dealt with Claire Morgan, the big Broadway star — not with Johnny Leinster, or even with June Henson, the darling of society in those far-off twenties.

One of the bottom drawers was locked but there was a key on the dressing table and I bent to fit it into the lock. Just as I was about to turn it, I heard a faint scraping behind me, as though a couple of mice were scrabbling at the rich red carpet. Only it wasn't mice. I tried to turn and get to my feet at the same time, only I wasn't quite quick enough.

Something battered down against the back of my neck and I lurched forward against the dresser. Somehow, I managed to break my forward fall with my elbows. I wriggled sideways and tried to roll out of the way of the second smash I guessed was on its way. It caught me a glancing blow on the side of the face and heaved me into the carpet.

Somebody swore softly under their breath, then a heavy blow licked me in the small of the back and it was all I could do to keep sucking air into my lungs and stop from screaming out loud with the pain of the blow.

Everything grew a little hazy. I tried to roll away again, to turn over on my back and get a glimpse of my attacker, but I couldn't move a muscle. Something heavy was standing in the small of my back and I felt a heel grinding into my spine, cutting through the cloth of my jacket.

Then something burst at the back of

my eyes. A grenade seemed to explode in my brain and I went all the way out. In a way, I was glad. It took the pain away and it was just like going to sleep.

8

Taken for a Ride

I woke up with my head throbbing like a drum. I dragged myself to my feet in pitch darkness. Then somebody switched on the light and I stood blinking at it before I could make out who stood in the doorway.

It was the bruiser from along the passage. Behind him, I caught a glimpse of blonde hair, and Sally Benton came into the room. They both had worried looks on their faces.

'Mike!' Sally ran forward and held me up by the arms. 'What happened?'

'That's some question,' I said, grinning weakly. 'The back of my head feels like a squashed tomato. Somebody slugged me over the head while I was trying the bottom drawer.'

'Did you get a good look at him?' the bruiser wanted to know.

I shook my head and my brain took another pounding. 'Not a glimpse. He must have been waiting in that other room for me. I locked the door behind me so he couldn't have come in from the passage.'

The bruiser went over to the smaller room and peered inside. I sat down shakily in a chair, facing the mirror. My face looked back at me from the glass.

The bruiser came back. 'Nobody in there now. He must have skipped out the door. It's a certainty he must have had a key to get in here in the first place.'

'I guess you're right. That should narrow down the field a bit.'

My back felt as though a steam hammer was battering at it continuously. I hoped my kidneys hadn't been smashed up too badly.

'But who could it have been?' Sally Benton looked at me for a long moment.

'Somebody who had the same ideas as myself, perhaps,' I told her. 'There's no sense in looking through this place now. Whoever slugged me will have got hold of anything that might have been important.'

I looked round at the bouncer. 'Thanks for the key,' I said. 'Any idea how long I was out cold?'

'Almost fifteen minutes, I'd guess, Mr. Torlin. When you didn't come back I thought something might have happened, and I was on my way here when this young lady turned up. She said she knew you, so I let her come.'

'Thanks.' I checked my watch but the face was smashed in and the hands had been shattered completely.

'Think you can stand up?' asked Sally. I winced. The room was still going round in the full circle and there was a pounding at the back of my skull that persistently refused to go away. I shut my eyes and opened them again. That made things a little better. The room steadied.

'Here, maybe a drop of brandy will help.' The big guy moved across into my line of vision and held out a flask.

'Thanks.' My voice sounded like a hoarse croak.

My fingers weren't too steady, and trying to keep the brandy in the flask only made them tremble more. Finally, I managed to take a couple of quick gulps of the raw spirit. It burned the inside of my mouth, but it stayed down and exploded in an expanding haze of warmth and comfort in the pit of my stomach.

With the brandy inside me I managed to stand upright and stay that way. I slipped behind the wheel of the Bentley and Sally Benton crushed into the seat beside me. My body felt as though it were on fire. My ribs creaked as I pressed the starter.

'I'll take you back to the carnival,' I said. 'Nearly time for the evening show.'

She nodded dismally. 'I heard about Pete,' she explained. 'Hammond told us that you were still on the case. I thought I'd find you at the theatre.'

'Sure. Claire Morgan was killed this morning. Did Hammond tell you that?'

She sat there, looking at me with a smoky expression in her eyes. I couldn't quite fathom the meaning behind it. 'No. I didn't know that,' she said finally. 'What happened?'

'Somebody had the clever idea of putting a live slug in the gun they use in the play. The poor guy who played the part of the husband pulled the trigger and shot her.'

'So it's another murder to chalk up along with the rest?'

I nodded and said in a low voice: 'I had an idea it might have been your boss who'd committed all these murders.'

She opened her mouth in surprise, then shut it again as I went on quickly. 'Yes, I know what you're going to say. That nobody in their right mind would deliberately ruin his own business, but there's one little point that Hammond rooted out that changed all that. It seems that Claire Morgan was blackmailing Donati with something she'd picked up from way back. If you'd asked me a couple of hours ago who the murderer was, I'd have said Donati. Now I've changed my mind.'

'Oh?' She sounded curious.

'Yeah. Because this afternoon I knew just where Donati was. He's still locked up in jail with Lieutenant Hammond watching him like a mother hen, so it wasn't him who slugged me in Claire

Morgan's dressing room.'

I pulled out into the main stream of cars and headed east towards the outskirts of town.

'Thank heaven that he didn't kill them.' The relief in Sally's voice was genuine.

I drove quickly, reaching the fairground in a little under fifteen minutes. It looked quiet enough on the outside, but I sensed that peculiar waiting quality again. Jane Knight and Carmen Phillips were already there. They said an affable 'hello' to me, then went into the room at the back to dress.

'Would you like a drink, Mike?'

'Thanks, Sally. I guess I could use one after that beating up. I doubt whether I've got a whole bone in my body.'

She went over to the table, slid back the front, took out a bottle and poured me a double Scotch. I drank it down in one gulp. 'Thanks,' I said. I lit a cigarette and looked down at my glass.

The two showgirls came out of the back room. There was a scared expression on Jane's face, but I didn't think of it at the time. I had too many other things on my mind.

No sooner had they gone than two tough-looking characters stepped in from the other room. They were both dressed in sober grey pin-striped suits. The only thing that marked them out from city bank clerks was the guns they carried in their hands. It made them look kind of sinister.

'I guess you're this guy Mike Torlin? That right, punk?' said the taller guy with the hatchet face.

'That's right,' I agreed.

'Who's the dame?' the other guy wanted to know.

'What's that to you?'

'Don't make things any harder on yourself, Torlin. We ask all the questions.'

'OK, go ahead,' I said. 'Just what is it you want to know?' I felt a healthy respect for the guns. These guys looked as though they were capable of pulling a murder just for the fun of it.

'Moose Madison sent us.'

'Madison?' I tried to look as though I'd never heard the name before, but the expression didn't register with either of the two hoodlums.

'You heard me, wise guy,' said the taller of the two hirelings. 'You're out of luck, lady.' He turned to where Sally Benton was standing near the door. 'A pity you joined up with this crumb of a private dick, because we'll have to take you for a ride as well.'

'She knows nothing about this business,' I said harshly.

'Nobody asked you, shamus.' The tall, mean-looking guy pushed his gun forward with an impatient gesture.

'Now, right away,' muttered the other guy. His voice sounded like gravel being dropped on to a corrugated iron roof. 'The boss wants to see you right away and when he says now, he means now.'

'OK.' I turned to Sally. 'Sorry about this,' I said, 'but there's nothing I can do about it. They've got the drop on us.'

'Now you're talking sense, shamus.'

I moved towards the door. The tall guy's voice grated in my ear. 'Don't try anything funny, buster. Remember there's a gun in your back. If you try to tip anybody off, your girlfriend gets it first, then you next.'

'I wasn't thinking of trying anything,' I said.

The other guy laughed and I could hear the sound of dirt being shovelled onto my coffin in his voice. We walked slowly out of the booth with the two hoodlums following in our shadows. There was a car at the back, a sleek black convertible. A thin, ferret-faced guy sat smoking behind the wheel. He tossed his cigarette out of the window as we appeared and pressed the starter.

'Inside,' gritted one of the hirelings.

Sally climbed into the back of the car and I followed. One of the hoodlums slid in beside me, while the other clambered into the front.

'OK Rudy, let her go.'

I said a mental goodbye to the Bentley and wished that Sally hadn't been in on this deal. It seemed that everybody I came into contact with became entwined in a mesh of disaster.

We hit the main street outside the fairground and the guy in the front seat slipped his gun back into his pocket; but the other, slouched in the seat beside me, kept his clutched in his fist. He grinned, and a slit appeared in the broken slab of concrete he had for a face. 'Say, Rudy,' he called harshly, 'this guy was pretty easy to take. Guess he knows what's good for him and doesn't want any trouble.' The guy behind the driving wheel grated a thin laugh, then concentrated on his driving.

I began to wish I'd thought more about what Johnny Leinster had told me. I was the chump for not heeding the warning he'd given me. I hadn't gotten around to checking on whether Moose Madison was in town. It was obvious now that he was, and had been for some time, otherwise he wouldn't have known about me. It didn't take him long to catch on.

We were now heading out of town along one of the freeways leading south. The convertible was doing somewhere in the region of sixty and I was beginning to hope that a couple of traffic cops might pop out of a side turning, when the hope died in me.

'Turn next at the crossroads, Rudy. We're taking them straight to the boss. He's expecting them.'

Rudy swung the wheel expertly and we drove into a narrow turning, almost hidden from the road. At the end of it, set behind a clump of trees, lay a small ranch house. We stopped on the gravel outside it and the big guy next to me got out and stood waiting for us to do likewise, the heavy gun still in his fist. The other hirelings climbed lazily out of the front seat and whispered something to Rudy; the latter nodded and drove the convertible off, somewhere round the rear of the ranch house.

'In here,' said the big guy.

'I hope the boss will forgive us for not being formally dressed,' I said pleasantly, hoping to rile him, 'but I think he'll understand we had very little notice of this visit.'

The granite features never changed. The small, mean eyes narrowed just a shade, the lids drooping lazily over them. I remembered seeing a cobra at the zoo once, and the look in the hoodlum's eyes sent little goose pimples popping up all over me. There was death at the back of his gaze.

'Don't make me kill you before I have to, Torlin,' he muttered finally, speaking from between his teeth. 'And remember, when that time comes, your girlfriend goes first, and it's going to give me the greatest pleasure to watch you both die.' He said it as though he meant it and I shivered again.

We went inside, under an upstairs veranda and through a long hall. There were tall flowers growing in pots along either side of it, giving the place an exotic look. Their heady perfume stung at my nostrils.

'Through here.' One of the bruisers pushed open a door and ushered us inside.

A tall, thin guy sat listening to a fight commentary on the radio. He had his back to us but there was something familiar about him that clicked into place in my brain. I tried to figure out where I'd seen him before, but at that moment he turned round and I knew.

'Thanks for dropping in like this, Torlin,' said Madison nasally. 'It's a pity it had to be this way, because now you know who I am, and that isn't healthy — for you.'

It was the thin, mean-looking guy I'd met in Pete Donati's office that first day he'd hired me. At first, it didn't figure. Then it made sense, real sense. This was Madison, the guy who'd worked with Leinster in the old days, back in the roaring twenties. But just as Leinster had changed his face and his identity, this guy must have been equally successful, maybe even more so, because it looked as though even his old boss from Prohibition days hadn't recognized him.

'That's right, Torlin. I figured you'd recognize me. Funny thing about Leinster. He may be a clever guy in a lot of ways, but he always seems to overlook the obvious. I've been working for him for over two years now, and he still doesn't know who I am.'

'He's bound to find out sooner or later,' I said, trying to speak calmly.

Madison laughed softly. 'So you really

100

think so? Don't be a fool all your life, Torlin. I've got away with it for two years; I think I'll manage it for all the rest of the time I'll need.' He switched off the radio with a slow, easy movement, then turned to look at the taller of the two hoodlums. 'OK, Clance,' he said sharply. 'You can go now, but get back here before ten. I may need you again for a little job I have in mind.'

'Right, boss.' The big guy opened the door and slipped out, closing it quietly behind him. A moment later, I spotted him walking across the lawn in front of the house.

Madison slewed round in his chair and sat watching me for a long moment, a faint sneering smile on his face. Then he rubbed his nose with the back of his hand and said nasally, 'Who's the dame, Mike? Somebody you got to know at the carnival?'

'That's none of your business, Madison,' I said, trying to look braver than I felt.

'Don't rile me, Torlin.' There was real menace in Madison's whining voice.

'Nobody tells me what's my business and what isn't. Get that?'

Something hit me at the side of the head and I went down on one knee. Sally gave a faint scream, then shut up as I staggered to my feet. The hireling was holding his bunched fist in the palm of his other hand and looking pleased with himself. He looked inquiringly at Madison.

Moose sneered up at me. His voice was expressionless as he said, 'I asked you who the dame was, Torlin.'

'She works at the carnival,' I said. There was a dull ringing in my head where the thug had hit me.

'That's nice,' said Madison. The big guy behind me laughed, and it was like glass scraping on gravel.

'She's got nothing to do with this,' I said evenly. 'Leave her out of it, Madison.'

'You're hopeful, Torlin.' Madison inspected his nails methodically. 'She's with you, isn't she? That way, I figure she knows more than is good for her, and I can't afford to take any more chances where you're concerned.'

'You've got this deal figured all wrong, Madison,' I told him. My legs were feeling shaky and there were a couple of sledgehammers beating a tattoo inside my brain.

He shook his head slowly. 'No, I don't think so. You were hired by Leinster to check on what's been happening out at the carnival — right?'

I nodded.

'And by now, he's around to pinning it on me — right again?'

'I wouldn't know about that,' I retorted.

'Like hell you don't.' His thin lips twisted into a warning sneer. 'What a sucker I was not to get you bumped off before. It would have saved me plenty of time and dough. You're pretty pally with Hammond of Homicide, aren't you?'

'That's right.' I nodded. 'He follows me closer than my own shadow. Maybe he's right outside now, watching this place, wondering what the hell I'm doing talking to Moose Madison.'

There was a little flicker of something in Madison's close-set eyes, but it wasn't fear. Maybe it was hate, I don't know. He grinned suddenly and shifted his thin frame more comfortably in the chair. 'The trouble with you, Torlin,' he said softly, 'is that you never know when you're licked. Now I want to know just how far you've got with this case.' His voice dropped a shade as he went on. 'And don't try any lies, because I don't like it.'

I'd always been taught to believe that the guy who has somebody behind you with a gun in his fist has the right to ask the questions and expect the right answers. It just isn't healthy to forget that rule. 'That's easy enough,' I said. 'I figured that Claire Morgan had something to do with the murder of Helen Crossman, otherwise she'd have turned up on schedule at Leinster's Easter party. When she didn't, I decided to take a trip out to the theatre and question her about it. Unfortunately for the Torlin luck, she copped a bullet during the rehearsals before I could get to her. If she'd talked I might have had something positive to go on.'

'Seems as though you've been clear out of luck from the very beginning, Torlin.' He looked at me. 'Though I did think you knew a bit more than that.'

'Oh, sure,' I said with sarcasm. 'If I'd known any more I wouldn't be here now with a bunch of cheap hoodlums.'

I saw the flush rising to Madison's thin face and he half-rose from his chair. I wanted to rile him just enough to get him to give me a little more information, but not enough to get myself killed.

'You'll regret that, Torlin,' he grated. The hatchet-faced guy came round from behind me. His left fist chopped out on my cheek, grazing the bone with the ring on his finger. A vicious kick hit me behind the knee, pitching me forward onto the carpet. I rolled a couple of times and got another kick in the side.

'OK, I think he's learned his lesson,' said Madison dispassionately.

I got up, feeling sick. Sally caught my arm and held me up.

'That was the hard way, Torlin,' said Madison softly. 'If you want to play it that way, just say something else.'

I shook my head. There was no future in it, I decided. Not if I wanted to stay healthy for a little while longer.

'OK.' Madison lit a cigarette and the end glowed redly as he sucked in his cheeks. 'Now I've got to figure out what to do with you. The dame complicates things, but I guess we can figure some way around that.'

'You'll never get away with it,' I warned him. 'Hammond isn't that much of a fool. He knows I'm on this case and no phoney suicide is going to put him off.'

Madison sneered again. 'I'm getting tired of hearing that, Torlin. There isn't going to be any suicide pact, no notes. Just two bodies in a car accident. Hammond can do what he likes with you then.'

9

Any More for Murder?

The hatchet-featured hoodlum fitted a silencer to his gun with an expert touch and clipped it, ready for use, into his pocket. Now I got it — we were going to be taken for a ride in the strictly old-fashioned way with no frills attached.

Somebody rapped on the door, then opened it. A slender, horse-faced guy came in. Behind him came Rudy.

'Get the car?' asked Madison.

Rudy nodded. 'It was easy enough,' he said. 'Nobody tried anything.'

Madison turned round and stood watching us for a moment. Then he nodded. 'OK, Rudy, take them as far as the main highway before you let them go. And don't forget the whisky.' He grinned as though amused at something.

We went outside and I saw my Bentley drawn up in front of the ranch house.

Rudy slipped in behind the wheel and the tall guy got in beside us in the back. The third hoodlum took the sleek convertible.

So we were going out to a nice quiet place to die. I tried to figure how they were going to do it. Any fake suicide and Hammond, even though he hated my guts, would start asking awkward questions and making awkward inquiries; and sooner or later they would reach back to Moose Madison, particularly if Leinster talked.

'If you think you can fake an accident, you're mistaken, Rudy,' I said loudly. But I didn't even convince myself.

The big guy laughed. 'You're still being a sucker, Torlin,' he grunted. 'The way we're going to fix this, not even your best friend will think it's murder.'

'OK,' I said, 'Just how do you figure on doing it?'

'That's easy. A chloroform pad to put you out, a bottle of whisky smashed over you while you're sitting behind the driving wheel with your girlfriend beside you, then we start the car and you hit the first lorry on the highway. If there's enough left of you for identification, they'll put it down to drunk driving.'

So that was it. No wonder Madison was sure Hammond wouldn't figure on murder. It was all so diabolically ingenious. There might be a few suspicions, but no proof.

'This is a lot better than killing you out of hand,' growled the hoodlum. 'But if you figure on running, see how far you get.'

We reached the end of the drive and stopped just beyond the edge of the highway. I had a quick look around as Rudy switched off the engine and got out. There was a heavy truck in the distance, but it was going away from us; and we could expect no help from that quarter, even if we could hope to attract the driver's attention.

'All right, shamus, into the driving seat,' ordered the hireling. He took out the gun with the silencer and pushed it forward threateningly. I got slowly out of the car and stood blinking in the sunlight. Sally got out behind me while Rudy stood watching with a hungry look on his face. I slid in behind the wheel and Sally joined me a minute later. There was a glazed expression in her eyes and I felt like a heel, just sitting there without trying something.

'That's better, shamus,' said the big guy. 'This is a lot better finish than you deserve. Pity the boss wouldn't let us kill you before — then we wouldn't have to go to all this trouble. No private dick's worth it.'

'Glad you think so,' I said slowly, forcing calmness into my tone.

I heard him laugh again, and then something was forced over my mouth and nostrils. There was a suffocating smell in my nose. All the breath seemed to have left my body, with only a vacuum in my lungs. Madly, I fought for breath and tried to claw at the cloth over my face. The hoodlum's laugh boomed louder and louder in my ears until it blotted out everything else.

Dimly, I was aware of the engine being started. Then something exploded in a haze of lights inside my brain and I dropped forward into darkness.

There was the raw stench of alcohol in my nostrils when I came round. The suffocating sensation was still in my lungs and I sucked in several mouthfuls of air. The dashboard was going round and round in a series of dizzying circles and I lifted a hand to my forehead.

It felt as though a concert of drums was beating an insistent refrain at the back of my temples. I tried to move my legs but something was pinning them down. That brought me to my senses right away. Little memory fragments started dropping into place, slotting themselves together in my head. Something dripped from my hair on to my lips and I tasted the raw sharpness of whisky.

I tried to roll over and free myself, but the steering wheel was hard up against my chest and Sally Benton lay hard against my free arm, her face bloody and twisted.

She was still breathing but I couldn't see how badly hurt she was. After what seemed a long time, I heard the sound of breaking glass close to my ear, and a rush of cold air hit me on the side of the face.

'Hell, another drunk,' I heard a disgusted voice say loudly.

I managed to turn my head. A traffic cop looked at me through the smashed window. I winced as I moved my head, then croaked my words out. 'Moose Madison,' I mumbled dully. 'He chloroformed us, then smashed a bottle of whisky inside the car to make it look like an accident.'

'Yeah, sure.' There was genuine disbelief in the other's sarcastic voice. 'That's what they all say. Surprising how many guys are framed on a charge like this.' He wrenched the door open and dragged me out. Then he went back for Sally.

'Is she OK?' I asked him.

'No, thanks to you.' He pulled back Sally's eyelid and looked closely. Then he glanced up at his companion and nodded. 'She'll live. Looks like a simple case of concussion to me.' He straightened and came across to me. 'Think you can stand, buster?' There was a faint trace of anger in his voice.

'I reckon so.' I staggered to my feet and remained upright.

'Good, because you're coming with me. I'm booking you for drunk driving. You can thank God you didn't hit anybody else on the road or you might have faced a manslaughter charge.'

'But you don't understand,' I protested.

'Don't make it any tougher on yourself than you have to, buster,' he said grimly. 'Shall we go?'

'What about her?' I asked.

'A fat lot you care!' muttered the other cop. 'I'll see she gets medical attention.'

I didn't like leaving Sally in that condition, particularly with Madison still somewhere in the vicinity, but I had no choice. It was more than my licence was worth to pull a fast one with the law.

'OK,' I said, 'you win.'

'We always do,' said the taller of the two cops. 'Let's move.'

At the station, I asked to be allowed to put a call through to Lieutenant Hammond. The desk sergeant looked a little bewildered at that, then decided it

113

wouldn't do any harm and gave a brief nod.

'Only make it short,' he said.

Hammond answered on the third ring. He sounded impatient.

'Yes?'

'Hammond?'

'That you, Torlin?'

'Yes. Now listen, Lieutenant. This is important. I don't know whether Leinster has talked any yet, but he warned me to be on the lookout for a cheap mobster called Moose Madison, one of his old associates.'

'So?' There was a spark of interest in Hammond's voice.

'Well, he ran into me. A couple of his boys were waiting for me at the carnival. They persuaded me to go with them to a ranch house somewhere off the north highway.'

'Go on.' I could almost hear Hammond's brain ticking over, filing everything I said away with a photographic precision, assessing every little inflexion of my tone. In a year's time he would be able to recall every little detail of this conversation, to pull it out of the adding machine that he had for a brain, and bring it all to light again.

'I had Sally Benton from the carnival with me. They put us both out with chloroform, brought my Bentley from the fairground, and smashed a bottle of whisky inside the car before sending it off along the highway.'

'So? What do you want me to do about it? Pull in this Moose Madison and charge him with attempted murder?'

'That's something that can wait,' I said. 'I'm at the 14th Street precinct. They're holding me on a charge of drunk driving. I thought maybe a word from you would clear me. It's important I get after this guy Madison. I figure he knows more than he ought to about this case.'

'Very funny,' he growled. There was a note of triumph in his low voice. 'I always figured you'd get yourself into a mess like this, Torlin, if I waited long enough.'

I waited until he tired himself out, then said, 'Try to see it my way. Madison and his bunch of hoodlums will skip that ranch house before your boys get within half a mile. They can smell a cop even when he's still over the horizon.'

There was a thoughtful pause. 'OK, Torlin. Get the sergeant on the phone. I'll see that you're released. By the way, what happened to the girl?'

'The traffic cop thinks she's just suffering from slight concussion. He seemed to figure she'd be OK. There's a doctor on the way already.'

'I get it,' Hammond growled.

I gave the phone to the desk sergeant and awaited events.

When the other finally replaced the phone in its cradle, there was a dazed expression in his eyes. He looked at me curiously for several seconds, then muttered, 'OK, Mr. Torlin, the lieutenant says you're free to go. But don't try anything else like this or you'll pay for it. OK?'

'You don't have to worry,' I told him, collecting my belongings. 'The next time, you'll have to worry about Madison, not me.'

I went out into the street and wondered how badly hurt Sally Benton had been. I didn't know too much, but things were beginning to slot themselves into a reasonable pattern. Previously, they had been nothing more than bits of a jigsaw scattered all over the place — some at the fairground, others at the theatre and in a small ranch house. Now there was a pattern behind them, but I was still worried. It wouldn't be long before Moose Madison and his bunch of thugs discovered that their little murder plot had failed, and they would be itching to do something more about it.

Next time, they might be a little more successful. I guessed they wouldn't fool around making it look like an accident again. When they got back on the ball it would be a slug in the back as far as I was concerned.

I had a quick look along the street, then started to walk towards the centre of town. I wanted to know how much Leinster had told his lawyer, and then I'd try the local hospital and ask about Sally Benton.

10

The Mouthpiece Talks . . .

I found Clive Rookman at his office. He eyed me suspiciously as I walked in, then motioned me towards a chair. I shut the door and sat down easily, feeling like Daniel thrown to the lions. Rookman was a shark and everybody seemed to know it except Leinster. Why he had engaged such a crooked lawyer in the first place, I couldn't figure.

'I understand you're representing Donati,' he said smoothly. 'As his lawyer I can only say that I doubt whether he will require your services. I don't think there's any doubt that he'll get off this rap.'

'You're kidding,' I said softly. 'Pete Donati — or Johnny Leinster, whichever you care to call him — is right on the hook. I've talked to Lieutenant Hammond since I last saw my client, and I think you're going to have a headache trying to spring him.'

Rookman smiled easily, but there was a nervousness behind the insistent drumming of his fingers on the top of the desk. 'I think I can manage my own affairs without any outside help, Mr. Torlin,' he said primly. 'This is an open-and-shut case. No jury would convict him if it ever came to the point of facing a trial.'

I looked at him. 'I suppose you know who he really is?'

'Johnny Leinster? Yes, I've known that for some time now. It doesn't pay to keep secrets from one's lawyer.'

'I guess not. Did he tell you that Claire Morgan was blackmailing him up to the hilt? That she'd been doing this for the past twenty years or so? Did he tell you that, Rookman?'

'Of course he did,' retorted the other defensively, but I could detect a note of anger in his voice and he didn't sound very sure of himself. I guessed that Johnny Leinster hadn't talked too much to Rookman during that interview in the cells. Maybe he had been waiting to see what I could dig up. Maybe he had figured that the fewer people who got to know about the blackmail the better. But I guessed that whatever the reason, this was the first that Clive Rookman had heard about it.

'Then if you knew that, why aren't you doing anything about it?' I asked.

'Such as?' He looked at me queerly.

'Never mind,' I said, grinning. 'I guess I'll have to do all the worrying as far as Johnny Leinster's concerned.'

He drew himself up to his full height and glared at me. His face was a study of mixed emotions. For a moment I thought he was about to explode, then he pulled himself together. 'For all I care, Mr. Torlin,' he said, with as much dignity as his outraged pride could muster, 'you can go to hell.'

I went out of the office and slammed the door. My visit to Clive Rookman hadn't proved too fruitful, but at least I'd got some things off my mind. I'd also given him something to worry about, a big headache that would make him earn his money. Rookman was as big a shark as many of the old-time mobsters. He made his money out of double-fast dealing and because he did it legally, I hated him more than people like Johnny Leinster.

Outside, I rang the east-side hospital and asked about Sally Benton. The day sister answered the phone. 'Miss Benton was admitted twenty minutes ago,' she said, and I could hear the starch crackling in her voice. 'She has slight concussion but should be up and about in a few days.'

'Any visitors allowed?' I wanted to know.

'Are you a relative of Miss Benton's?' parried the day sister.

I told my first big lie of the day. 'That's right,' I said, without hesitation. 'Her brother. When can I see her?'

'This evening at seven thirty.'

'That'll suit me fine,' I said and hung up.

Back at the office, I dug into the bottom drawer of my desk and brought out the Luger. It wasn't loaded, but I clicked a full magazine into it and slipped a spare into my pocket. There was no doubt in my mind that Moose Madison and his hoodlums were playing for keeps. The Luger made me feel a little better. Maybe they had me figured for a sucker with more lives than a cat. But next time, I was determined that they would be on the wrong side of a gun. Then I'd be in the position of being able to ask the questions.

I picked up my hat from the desk, stuck it on my head, and went out. On the way downtown, I bought myself a watch to replace that which had been smashed in Claire Morgan's dressing room. Buying it made me think about her, and the more I did so the more complicated things became. It was there, I felt sure, that the answer to this whole business lay, if I could only see it.

I went inside a small restaurant, sat down at the bar and ordered toast, bacon and eggs, and orange juice. The place was still half-empty but filling rapidly as the evening crowds came in — some of them on their way to the theatres, cinemas and bowling alleys; others to watch the fights and wrestling downtown. I kept my eyes open for any of Moose Madison's hirelings, watching the door through the glass mirror at the back of the bar. Very soon, they would be roaming the streets of Chicago, hoping to get the drop on me. Moose would be pretty mad by now, and I could imagine that somebody might get into a hell of a lot of trouble when Madison was mad.

I was just beginning to think that it was time to go over to the hospital and see Sally Benton, when the door was pushed open and Carmen Phillips came in. She was wearing a flame-coloured dress under a knee-length coat and the whole ensemble seemed to cling to her figure as though she had been poured into it.

She saw me instantly and sat down on the stool beside me. 'I've been looking for you all over town,' she said breathlessly. 'I heard what happened with those hoodlums.'

'Oh?' I tried not to sound too interested. 'Who told you about that?'

She laughed nervously and leaned her elbows on the bar. 'Lieutenant Hammond was down at the fairground just over an hour ago, checking on Jane and myself.

We told him everything we knew about those two men in the back room. He told us you'd managed to get away.'

I nodded and ordered her a drink. She gulped it down quickly when it arrived and held the empty glass out towards the bartender. 'Another one, please,' she said.

The bartender took the glass from her, refilled it and handed it back.

'Shouldn't you be back at the fairground, Carmen?' I asked.

She shook her head. I guessed from her actions that she was already a little high. She giggled thinly. 'We're all out of a job for the time being. The lieutenant closed the carnival until further notice.'

'I see.' I wondered why he had done that. Whether it was because Leinster was in jail, or because he didn't want any further accidents breaking out. It was impossible to figure out what might be in Hammond's mind, so I gave it up in disgust. 'What did you want to see me about, Carmen?' I asked, swivelling round on my stool to look at her more closely. 'Surely not just to inquire about my health?'

She bit her lower lip. 'Not exactly. I guess I was wrong in keeping things back from you. Maybe if I'd told you what I knew, this wouldn't have happened.'

'OK,' I said. 'What is it you should have told me?'

'The night when Helen was murdered, I wasn't able to get to the party in time.' She shuddered, then went on. 'And I'm rather glad I didn't. I was outside among the crowds and saw you come out. I guessed something was wrong when I saw Lieutenant Hammond arrive, but I didn't know what it was exactly.'

'So you saw me come out of the tent after the murder,' I said. My mind was on other things, but it was jerked back to reality by Carmen Phillips' next words.

'That's right. I was coming across to ask you what had happened when I saw somebody on the roller coaster, watching you.'

I grabbed her arm and felt my fingers bite into the flesh. 'Did you see who it was?' I asked urgently.

She nodded. 'Yes, quite clearly.' Her voice seemed to have lost some of its warmth. 'It was Claire Morgan.'

'Claire Morgan!' This time my surprise was really genuine. 'Are you sure?'

'I'm positive. I could see her quite clearly in the light from the big tent. There was no mistaking her.'

'But that doesn't make sense. Why should Claire Morgan want to kill me?'

'I'm sure I don't know.' Carmen Phillips shrugged her shoulders. 'I thought you ought to know. After she'd dropped that lump of stone on top of where you were standing, I saw her running along the edge of the roller coaster. Then she crouched down behind two of the supports and I didn't see her again for several minutes. During that time, you'd left.'

'What did she do then?' I asked harshly.

'She climbed down from the supports and ran towards the entrance to the fairground. I caught a glimpse of her getting into a car and driving off, but I couldn't see whether she was alone or not.'

'It's highly likely she was,' I said bitterly. There was only one other question. 'Did you ever see Claire Morgan around the carnival before that day? I mean, did she ever visit Pete Donati?'

'Yes,' she said firmly. 'I saw them together once or twice, whenever Claire Morgan visited Chicago. Pete used to tell us she worked on the stage out east. I've no proof of course, but I gained the impression that they weren't on as good terms with each other as Donati would have liked us to think they were.'

I smiled bitterly, then got to my feet. 'Thanks a lot for telling me this, Miss Phillips,' I said. 'What you've told me has proved extremely helpful. It's upset a few of my ideas, but at least it's put some things in their proper perspective.'

'That's all right.' She smiled. 'I'm so glad I could help.'

'Just one thing more,' I said. I'd almost forgotten. 'Would you do something for me?'

She smiled lazily. 'Anything, Mr. Torlin.'

I could see that the Mike Torlin personality was beginning to pay off dividends. 'Keep your eye on the fairground if you can and let me know the minute any strangers turn up. Not Hammond and his retinue of cops, but other guys who might look like phoney inspectors or something of the sort. Will you do that for me, Carmen?'

She hesitated for the barest moment, then nodded. There was a puzzled expression in her eyes. 'I don't quite see why anybody should try to get into the fairground now that it's closed,' she said, pursing her lips, 'but if it'll help to get the murderer of Helen Crossman, I'll do it.'

'Good girl,' I said warmly.

I drank the last of the orange juice and walked out into the street. Out of the corner of my eye, I saw Carmen Phillips hurrying away through the early evening crowds. Then she disappeared from sight and I turned and caught a streetcar for the hospital.

When I arrived, I discovered that Sally already had a visitor. Lieutenant Hammond turned idly in his chair and regarded me with a sour smile. 'I understood that our agreement was that you would keep me informed of everything that happened,' he said harshly.

'So?' I murmured, sitting down beside the bed.

'So what do I find? You go snooping around in Claire Morgan's dressing room, get yourself slugged over the head and then get picked up by a bunch of hoodlums headed by Johnny Leinster's first lieutenant of the old days, Moose Madison.'

'Ah, so you've already met Moose,' I said affably.

He glared at me. 'Don't try to get funny again, Torlin,' he snapped. 'Remember, what I said earlier still goes. I can bust you and take you into court as a material witness, and your licence won't last long after that.'

'OK, Lieutenant.' I held up a soothing palm. 'Let me try to explain. Sally here and I had no idea those two bruisers were waiting for us in the fairground. Do you think we'd have walked into their trap if we did?'

'No, I suppose not,' he admitted grudgingly. 'But you could have told me about searching Claire Morgan's dressing room. What did you expect to find there?'

'Certainly not a bump over the head,' I muttered.

'Never mind about the jokes,' he said venomously. 'Just spill it.'

I shrugged. 'I wanted to know what Claire Morgan had on Johnny Leinster so that she could blackmail him successfully for twenty years. It had to be something pretty hot for her to get away with it all that time. Any other dame who tried it would have been found in the river with a slab of concrete around her legs.'

'Did you find anything?'

I shook my head. 'Nothing,' I said. 'One of the bottom drawers of her dresser was locked and I thought I'd found the key. I was just going to open it when the ceiling fell in and hit me on the back of the head.'

'Very funny,' snarled Hammond. He got up and stood glaring down at me for a long moment. Then he crushed his hat on to the top of his head and stalked out of the ward.

I turned to Sally Benton. 'You all right, Sally?' I asked.

She nodded. 'The doctor says I'll be up in two or three days,' she said.

'They've closed the fairground for the time being,' I told her. 'I had Carmen in to see me just a few minutes ago. Either Hammond's scared there'll be more accidents around the place, which means that he doesn't seriously think that Leinster had anything to do with them, or he figures he's got enough evidence to send him to the chair.'

'What do you think, Mike?'

'Me? I never know what Hammond's thinking. He's a cute guy for a cop. Deep. But I've got an idea in my mind that he's had second thoughts about your boss. Could be he figures he's innocent, but he's keeping him locked away in jail, hoping that the real murderer will show his hand.'

11

Conflicting Evidence

It was late when I finally got back to the office. I switched off the light and sat by the window, smoking. As far as I could tell, the case was beginning to slip slowly out of my grasp. Earlier that morning, I'd thought I'd got it all sewn up. But a lot of things had happened since then. The most peculiar part about the whole affair was that Madison hadn't yet made his play. I'd expected him at the office several times, either to ring the place and see if I'd got back, or to send a couple of his hired killers round with orders to finish me for good; but for some reason known only to himself, he was holding off.

I guessed it was time I pushed him into a wrong move. Reaching out for the phone, I spun the dial six times and listened. The line purred for a few moments before he answered.

'Moose Madison?' I said softly.

I could hear his harsh breathing on the other end of the wire, then his voice came over harshly. 'Who's that speaking?'

'Can't you guess,' I said gently. 'This is Mike Torlin. The guy you tried to kill this afternoon. Say, that was some accident you rigged up for us. Pity it didn't come off. But then, you can't allow for everything.'

'What the hell — '

'Now, Madison,' I said, 'try to control yourself. And speaking of accidents, I suppose you considered yourself a little more successful with those you engineered at Leinster's fairground. It was you who planned all those to put Johnny out of business, wasn't it?'

'I don't know what you're getting at, Torlin.' His voice sounded tinny and far away. 'But you're right off the beam. All I was interested in was getting rid of you permanently. Maybe I slipped up a little this afternoon, but next time there won't be any mistake.'

'Somehow I don't think there'll be a next time, Madison. You're not so sure of yourself now, are you? You'd like to know how much I've discovered and how much I've told Hammond.'

'Damn you, you'll regret this, Torlin,' he snarled. 'I promise you that.'

'Before you go on,' I interrupted, 'perhaps I ought to tell you that I've placed two sealed letters in a strong box with instructions that they go to Lieutenant Hammond if any accident happens to me. They contain dynamite, those papers, and I'm sure you wouldn't want them to fall into the wrong hands. The same goes for Sally Benton too.'

'So you think you've got everything sewn up pretty neatly, do you, Torlin?' he rasped.

'I think so,' I said, speaking confidently.

'I wouldn't bank on it,' he retorted. The line went dead and I guessed he was pretty mad. I wouldn't have liked to have been in Rudy's shoes or any of the other hoodlums' for that matter.

I replaced the phone and finished my cigarette. Outside, it was dark and the neon lights of Chicago formed a great coloured ribbon across the near horizon.

Somewhere out there, I reflected, would be Madison and his men, smarting under my escape, determined to do something about it. Whether or not Madison had believed my story about the papers in a safe deposit box, I didn't care.

For a while I sat by the half-open window watching the crowds on the street below. No sign of any of the hoodlums. I checked the Luger. If they came, I would be ready for them this time. I yawned. Locking the office door, I stretched myself out on the couch and closed my eyes. Somewhere in the distance a clock gonged eleven times. Then I was asleep.

When I awoke, it was nearly dawn. A few of the bright lights of Chicago were still flashing on and off monotonously in the distance, but there was already a greyness creeping over everything, dimming them. I got up and poured myself a stiff bourbon. It washed some of the cotton wool out of my mouth and woke me up completely. I slipped on my jacket and put the Luger in the pocket. Then I felt ready for anything.

There were still a lot of questions I

wanted to ask, and I figured I knew some of the people who might be able to answer them. I caught a glimpse of my face in the mirror on the way out, and decided that nobody would talk to me in that condition. Taking off my coat again, I hung it over the back of a chair, washed my face in a bowl of cold water, and plugged in the electric razor. Five minutes later I felt fresher, able to face another day.

I got a cab uptown to the theatre in which Claire Morgan had met her death. It dropped me off at the side entrance and I looked at my watch. It was nine fifteen — early for the place to be open, but I decided to risk it rather than hang around the joint, kicking my heels when there was work to be done.

I found the tall bruiser of the previous day still there. He looked as though he hadn't moved from the spot where I'd seen him nearly twenty-four hours earlier.

'You again,' he said, looking mildly surprised. 'I thought you'd have had enough of this place by now.'

'Not quite,' I answered him. 'There are

one or two things I'd like to know. Is the props guy around yet?'

'Stevens?' The bruiser shook his head. 'He doesn't usually turn up until ten.'

'I see. OK if I wait for him? It's important.'

'I'm not so sure. This place is still closed and we had Lieutenant Hammond of Homicide down yesterday evening in a roaring temper. He threatened me with my job if I let you in again without his say-so.'

'Will fifty bucks cover it?' I asked.

He licked his lips and I could see he was tempted. Then he seemed to reach a decision and shook his head.

'Seventy-five,' I said.

'OK. But make it snappy when Stevens comes, won't you. Losing my job here isn't worth seventy-five dollars.'

'I work fast,' I promised him. 'Fifteen minutes is all I want with him. Maybe less. It just depends how cooperative he decides to be. He may have to be persuaded.'

The props man turned up on the dot at ten o'clock. He was a small, scared-looking guy with dark hair that fell untidily over his forehead. I couldn't see him holding out long under grilling, but you could never tell.

'Somebody to see you, Carl,' said the bruiser. The little guy looked up as though expecting to see a gun pointing at his ribs. When he saw me, he looked even more scared. Maybe he had me figured as a cop.

'What do you want to see me for, mister?' he whined. 'I ain't done nothing.'

'Maybe,' I said. 'But I'd like to talk with you in private.'

'Are you a cop?' he asked suspiciously.

I shook my head. 'Nothing like that,' I said. 'I'm just interested in this case. I think you might be able to help me.'

'A newspaper guy?' he wanted to know, leading the way along the passage backstage.

'Something like that,' I reassured him. 'But don't worry. Nothing will be printed unless you give me the OK.'

He took me inside a small room filled to the ceiling with bits of junk. There were old masks and pistols lining the walls and bits of scenery propped up in odd corners. He sat down in an old cane chair and waved his right hand towards a second. I sat down and offered him the packet of cigarettes. He took one with a nod and inhaled deeply as I lit it for him.

'Now,' I began, exhaling a cloud of smoke. 'I suppose you know plenty about this wretched business of Claire Morgan. She was one of the greatest actresses of our time. It seems such a pity that she should have died like that. It was an accident, of course.'

I watched him narrowly. He grasped at the straw like a drowning man. 'That's right. An accident.' The words came bubbling out of him like a torrent.

'Any idea how that live slug could have got into the gun?' I asked.

The tip of his cigarette waxed and waned redly as he puffed at it nervously. There was a shifty expression in his eyes.

'None at all,' he answered finally. He stared down at his shoes and I couldn't see his face clearly, but I knew that he was lying.

'You're sure?'

'Of course I'm sure. Do you think I put

it there, intending to kill her?' His voice had grown louder and louder until he was almost shouting.

'Calm down, Mr. Stevens,' I said soothingly. 'I'm not here to pin a murder on you. All I want to do is to get at the truth as far as possible. You handled that gun. According to the police, your fingerprints were on it, together with that guy who played the part of Claire Morgan's husband in the play.'

'I suppose they were,' he said weakly.

'But you still don't know how that live slug could have got into the gun?'

He shook his head. 'If I knew that I would have told the cops, wouldn't I?' he said.

'Isn't it your duty to check all these things?' I went on, speaking relentlessly.

He seemed to sag slowly. 'I suppose so.' His voice seemed to tremble slightly. 'I'm sorry, I guess I haven't been thinking too clearly since it happened. I've been cross-examined by the police until I don't know what I'm saying.' He was really worried now; scared.

'That's all you've got to say?' I

muttered, standing up and moving towards the door.

He nodded his head slowly. 'That's all there is I can tell you. I'm pretty positive that it wasn't a live slug when I got that gun ready for the rehearsal. Somebody must have taken the blank out and slipped the cartridge in afterwards.'

'And you think that's possible? Could anybody have got hold of that gun after you'd made it ready, without you seeing them?'

'The guy who pulled the trigger could,' said the little guy as another thought struck him. 'He had it in his hand most of the time. He had plenty of opportunity for switching the blank.'

'It's certainly a thought,' I said wearily. I opened the door, then turned. 'Just one other point. Any idea who Miss Morgan's doctor was while she was in Chicago?'

The little guy looked up. His face was drawn and haggard, and he looked as though he'd just seen a ghost. For a moment, I thought he wasn't going to speak, then he nodded and said softly, 'Doc Rayburn. You'll find him in his surgery over on Twenty-Second Street.'

'Thanks.' I went outside and closed the door on him.

Outside in the street, I figured that maybe the seventy-five bucks had been money well spent after all. I was almost certain that the little guy had been lying when he'd claimed that he didn't know who had switched the bullets in the murder weapon. But he was scared stiff of something, or someone. And that set me thinking about Moose Madison again. Maybe he was in on this deal, but he'd have to wait for a little while; there were other things I wanted to know.

I hailed a cab and told the driver to take me to Twenty-Second Street.

12

End of an Act

Doc Rayburn's secretary was a small, petite brunette who flashed me a welcoming smile as I went in. She looked efficient too.

'Good morning,' I said. 'I'd like to see the doctor, if he isn't too busy.

'Are you one of his patients?' she asked.

I shook my head. 'We have — or at least we had — a mutual acquaintance,' I explained. 'Miss Claire Morgan. That's why I'm here.'

'I see.' She looked down at my card and the smile on her pleasant features became a little fixed and strained. 'I'll see if the doctor can see you now. You'll understand that he's a very busy man.'

'Naturally,' I said.

She got up and walked across the office towards a glass-panelled door. Knocking, she went inside and closed it gently behind her.

Two minutes later she reappeared. One pencilled eyebrow was raised half an inch. She looked like a woman who had just learned something she had never suspected.

'Doctor Rayburn will see you now, Mr. Torlin,' she said politely. 'Just go straight in.'

'Thanks,' I said.

Rayburn turned out to be a short, kindly-looking guy in his late forties. He got up from behind his desk and extended a hand towards me. 'In what way can I help you, Mr. Torlin?' he asked, sitting down.

Without preamble, I said, 'I understand you were Claire Morgan's doctor whenever she was in town?'

'That's right. She's consulted me on several occasions.'

'Can you tell me anything about her? Did she seem to have anything on her mind? Was she afraid of anyone?'

He smiled a tight-lipped smile. 'I can see you've been reading the daily newspapers, Mr. Torlin,' he said gently.

'I'm afraid they exaggerate these things to a very great extent.'

'Maybe so,' I said, somewhat impatiently, 'but I was there when Claire Morgan was shot. As you'll see from my card, I'm a private detective. I've been hired to investigate this case, and anything you can tell me which might have a possible bearing on it will be of considerable help to me.'

He sat silent for a long moment, his fingertips placed together in front of him, his elbows resting on the top of the desk. There was a glint of malicious humour in his eyes and something else I couldn't quite identify.

'You think she was murdered, Mr. Torlin?'

I nodded. If he was to be frank with me, it was only fair that I should lay all my cards on the table. 'I'm quite positive she was murdered, doctor,' I said. 'But unfortunately at the moment I'm not quite sure who did it, and I certainly lack the necessary proof to convict them.'

'I'm beginning to see the extent of your problem. But you put me in a very delicate position. As you know, the case histories of all our patients are confidential. They have to be for various reasons.'

'I realize that, doctor,' I said urgently. 'But in a case such as this, couldn't you possibly stretch a point?'

'I'm not sure whether it would help you very much, Mr. Torlin,' he said ponderously. He ran his hand over his rapidly balding head.

'Anything can help in a case like this,' I said, 'and you'll have had the satisfaction of knowing that you'd helped to bring a malicious murderer to justice.'

He appeared to ponder that statement for a long moment, then he nodded as he reached a decision. 'Very well. In these circumstances, I think there may be something I can tell you. Just one moment.' He flicked across the switch of the office intercom and waited.

'Yes, doctor?' the brunette's voice said tinnily.

'Get me the file on Miss Morgan, will you, Anne.'

'Right away, Doctor.'

A minute later, she came into the

surgery with the slender dossier containing the case history of Claire Morgan.

'That will be all for the moment, Anne,' said Rayburn quietly.

She went out of the room and closed the door behind her. Doctor Rayburn opened the folder on his desk and thumbed through the papers inside. He was silent for a while, his face showing mixed emotions. Then he looked up and said quietly, 'Miss Morgan came to me a little over two years ago, Mr. Torlin. She had already seen a specialist in New York. I decided to keep her under constant observation. She visited me almost every fortnight.'

I sat straight in my chair at that and looked interested. 'What was it, doctor?' I asked. 'Anything serious?'

He nodded, his lips pursed into a thin, hard line across the middle of his features. He closed the folder with a sharp movement. 'Miss Morgan was suffering from a rare form of blood disease,' he said with an ominous quietness. 'There is no known cure and she was rapidly getting worse.'

I had expected something to click into place in my brain, but it didn't. Instead, I said, 'Just how bad was she, doc?'

Rayburn looked down at the closed folder on the desk in front of him. I couldn't see his eyes. Then he murmured softly, 'She had only another two or three months to live at the most, perhaps considerably less. We couldn't tell for certain.'

'Are you sure? There couldn't have been anything wrong with your diagnosis?'

'Not a chance, Mr. Torlin,' he said emphatically. 'My observations were confirmed entirely by the New York specialist.'

'So that was it,' I murmured softly. I sank back in my chair. My brain was ticking over like greased lightning. Things were happening a little too quickly to be taken in fully, but I tried to grasp the significance of this new development.

'One more question, Doctor. Did Claire Morgan know this, or did you keep it from her?'

'I told her myself three weeks ago. She wanted to know; said she could take it,

148

whatever the verdict was. Somehow, I thought she seemed rather glad when she knew the worst.'

'Only three weeks to live,' I said, half to myself. 'Three months, if she was really lucky. That's what I call a death sentence.'

'She took it quite well,' persisted Rayburn, looking at me over his rimless glasses.

'She was an actress,' I told him. 'She could quite easily have disguised her true feeling. After years on the stage, you get that way.'

'There's something hard and callous about you, Mr. Torlin, that I don't like,' said Rayburn.

'In my business, you see so many rotten things that you have to be callous,' I told him. I got to my feet. 'Thanks for the information anyway, doc. You've been a great help. I wonder if the murderer knew this?'

Rayburn shrugged. 'Would it have made any difference?' he said, placing the folder on Claire Morgan to one side. 'The only thing I can say is, that if he did, it wouldn't really have been murder, would it?'

'She was shot, Doctor,' I reminded him, 'and that's murder in the eyes of the law, whatever the motives might be behind it. Would she have been in any pain at the end?'

'A little, perhaps. But we could have prevented that with morphia.'

'Yes,' I agreed. 'I suppose you could. Anyway, thanks again, doc.'

He nodded and I opened the door and went out into the other office. The brunette looked up from her typewriter as I walked past. There was a faint smile on her lips, but that was all — although I could feel her eyes boring into the back of my neck as I walked out.

Little thoughts were having a fine time scampering around the edges of my brain. Just where did this last bit of information fit into the general scheme of things? It was a question I couldn't answer.

I called the hospital on the way back to the office and they told me that Sally would be leaving the following day. She had said for me not to worry and not to get into any further trouble.

After that, I went back into the small

restaurant I had visited the previous day and ordered a three-course lunch. My watch said fifteen minutes past eleven, but I still felt hungry and I realized that I hadn't eaten all day.

★ ★ ★

I was on the point of calling for the check when a thick-set character came thumping into the restaurant, spotted me in an instant and sat down at the table.

'A little bird told me I'd find you here,' said Hammond thickly.

'Now, Charles,' I said in an injured tone. 'Can't a guy eat a meal in a restaurant without being picked on by Homicide?'

'Cut the wise-cracks,' he said hoarsely, glaring at me from beneath thick black eyebrows. 'I figured that if I want any information from you, I'd better come and get it myself.'

'Sure,' I said slowly. 'First thing I found out was that Sally Benton will be released from hospital tomorrow. Apparently that bump on the head didn't shake her up as badly as they thought at first.'

'I heard about that,' Hammond said drily. 'Go on. Anything else?'

'That depends on what particular aspect of the case you're interested in,' I parried.

'You know damned well what I'm talking about,' he snarled. 'You were followed to Doctor Rayburn's surgery half an hour ago. Now, suppose you tell me why you went there? What did you expect to find out from him?'

'OK, Charles,' I said finally. 'I suppose I'd better tell you everything.'

'That's right,' he growled. 'You'd better if you value your licence.'

'I wanted to check up on Claire Morgan's health during the past few years. Carmen Phillips, one of the showgirls from the carnival, came to me yesterday with the news that it was Claire Morgan who'd been on that roller coaster, dropping lumps of stone onto guys like me underneath. I figured that if I saw her doctor, he might be able to confirm whether Claire was in any fit condition to go climbing around on roller coasters with lumps of stone weighing a little over twenty pounds.'

'I see.' Hammond looked interested. 'And did you find anything out from Rayburn?'

I nodded. 'Yes, but it wasn't exactly what I'd anticipated. He told me that she'd been suffering from some blood disease for the past three years or so. Apparently some specialist in New York confirmed this and Claire was told three weeks ago that she had only a couple of months to live. That there was nothing they could possibly do for her.'

Hammond stroked his chin. He smiled, without malice. 'Now that's better, Mike,' he muttered. 'At least, we're getting somewhere.'

I raised my eyebrows. 'But it still doesn't give us a clue to the murderer,' I said.

'You think this guy Madison might have had anything to do with it?' he asked sharply.

'Could be,' I replied. 'He and Leinster and Claire Morgan were all together during the thirties. It's a long time to harbour a grudge, I know, but it isn't really impossible.'

'I'm beginning to get the idea,' muttered Hammond softly. There was a faint gleam in his eyes. 'As I remember it from the records, Leinster ran out on the others when the big clean-up in Chicago started. Madison was left high and dry with a twenty-year rap ahead of him if I remember rightly. That could explain why he's out to get Leinster.'

'When did Madison get out of San Quentin?' I asked. 'Any idea?'

'Yeah. A couple of months ago. We heard he was heading for Chicago, but we had nothing on which we could hold him.'

'And Claire Morgan? I wonder why she was bearing a grudge?'

Hammond smiled grimly. 'Isn't it obvious?' he said.

'I guess I must be pretty dense this morning,' I said slowly.

'Hell, man. She must have been in love with this guy, Leinster, back in those days. I can't see any other reason why a high-class dame, the daughter of the mayor, living in the circles of high society, should team up with a cheap hoodlum like Johnny Leinster.'

'And when the clean-up started, he turned her down flat, is that it?'

'Well it fits the facts as we know them, doesn't it?' murmured Hammond, leaning back in his chair.

I nodded and had to admit to myself that he was right, for perhaps the first time in his entire career.

13

A Dame in Distress

Two days later I got around to having a second, closer look at the fairground. As Carmen Phillips had said, it was closed, and most of the staff seemed to have been paid off. There was one solitary guy standing outside the entrance. He eyed me suspiciously as I approached. Then his lips tightened as he had me figured for some reporter snooping around for a story. 'Looking for somebody, buster?' he asked.

'Not exactly,' I said complacently. 'I understand the carnival's been closed down by Lieutenant Hammond's orders.'

'That's right — and it's my business to see that it stays shut down. Nobody's allowed inside.'

'Better ring Hammond and see if he changes his mind,' I said softly. 'Because I'm going in.'

His jaw dropped suddenly, then his eyes narrowed and he said sharply, 'Listen, buster, I don't allow any third-rate reporter to talk to me like that. I've got a good mind to — '

'I'm not here looking for trouble,' I told him calmly, 'but I think you'd better get on the phone and tell Hammond that Mike Torlin's here and he wants to take a look around. OK?'

The guy took another long look at me, then shrugged his shoulders. 'OK, buster,' he called over his shoulder as he walked towards the booth. 'But if this is some kind of stunt, you'll regret it.'

I waited, listening patiently as he dialled a number on the phone. For a moment, I could hear the low murmur of conversation, then the thin ring as he put the phone back in its cradle. He came outside again and looked like a man who had just seen some wonderful revelation. 'Sorry I got so tough just then,' he said quietly. 'But we get so many reporters around here, trying all kinds of stories to get inside.'

'Don't apologize,' I said. I went inside,

leaving him standing open-mouthed at the gate. Reaching the entrance to the roller coaster, I started to climb up the wooden supports. Below, the ground looked a tremendous distance away, and the higher I went the more I could see.

Ten minutes later, I stood on top of the undulating rails of the roller coaster. The empty cars stood at the end. Down below, there was no one — not even a barker, shouting at the customers to take a ride in the ghost train. I could feel the sweat streaming off my forehead as I started along the dipping track. I walked forward several paces, clinging desperately to the protecting rail, wondering if anybody had been there a second time and sawn through the woodwork.

At the top of the second hump, I located the place where the accident of a few days earlier had occurred. I went down on one knee, locking my heels in the rail. The woodwork had been newly painted, but I could see where the fine teeth of the saw had bitten into the wood. Peering over the edge, I decided it was one hell of a drop, and that whoever had sawn through that wood hadn't wanted the guy who'd leaned on it to stand much chance of living.

I stepped back onto the rails, but the next minute something hiccoughed below me, and a section of the wooden rail splintered into chips. There was another faint pop, scarcely audible, and another bullet embedded itself in the wooden supports. I took a jump to the other side and crouched as low as I could against the metal rails. Whoever was down there taking pot shots at me was well hidden. Peering through the openings in the woodwork, I couldn't see anybody moving around. Even the guy at the entrance who'd let me in under protest had disappeared.

I had a quick look round, then started to crawl along the roller coaster. It didn't matter which way I went, I would still have to expose myself to the unseen gunman below. This was, perhaps, the time when heroes are made, but unfortunately I'm no hero. All I wanted to do was to get a glimpse of the guy who was firing at me and put a couple of slugs into him.

I didn't need to see him to know that it was one of Moose Madison's hirelings. They'd sworn to kill me, and this time Moose wouldn't listen to any excuse. Halfway down the steep slope of the roller coaster, I heard the faint plop of a silencer from almost directly underneath me. The bullet hammered into the woodwork less than two inches from my outstretched hand.

That settled it. I pulled out the Luger, checked the magazine, then leaned forward and pushed it cautiously between the woodwork. I saw the vague form of a guy in a broad-brimmed hat some thirty feet below me. For an instant, I glimpsed his upturned face, then I squeezed the trigger and felt the Luger jump back against my wrist with the recoil. The figure stumbled and fell on to its knees. I fired again just to be on the safe side.

Gingerly, I edged my way down the rearing structure of the roller coaster, dropping the last couple of feet. I ran up to the guy and pulled him over on to his back. There was a dark deep purple hole under his left eye that had finished it for him. He wasn't pretty, and I shivered a little as I realized the odds that were stacked against me. Moose Madison wouldn't rest once he heard about this.

Two minutes later, the tall guy from the booth at the fairground entrance made his appearance and stood looking down at the body. He looked round at me defensively. 'I thought I heard shots. What happened?'

'This punk started slinging lead at me while I was up there on the roller coaster,' I said shortly. I didn't feel like giving him all the sordid details, but Hammond might be mad enough to pull him in as a material witness and it wouldn't do to alienate him from the very beginning.

'Any idea who he is?'

I nodded briskly. 'He's one of Moose Madison's hired killers,' I explained. 'They tried to kill me a couple of days ago, only it didn't quite pan out as they'd expected. I guess he must have followed me here to finish the job.'

The tall guy chuckled softly. 'He didn't get very far, did he?'

I straightened up wearily. I had just

killed a man and I felt sick and dizzy inside. 'I'll have to call the cops, I guess,' I said. 'Even if he is a killer, he's dead and I shot him. Will you be around when they get here?'

He looked dubious, then nodded slowly. 'I suppose so. But I don't know anything about it if they start asking questions.'

'Just play dumb,' I told him. 'Lieutenant Hammond knows I'm here. He'll put two and two together and come up with the obvious solution.'

'All right,' he said. 'I'll wait for them. You're sure there aren't any more of them hanging around the place?'

It was a thought that hadn't struck me. I pursed my lips, then shook my head. 'I doubt it, somehow. If there were, they'd have tried to kill me before now.'

I left him beside the body, went back into the booth at the entrance and dialled the cops. I told the guy on the other end of the line to pick up a dead hoodlum underneath the roller coaster at Donati's Amusement Park. Then I hung up before the startled guy could asking any questions. After that, I decided to call Moose Madison. It would cost me a nickel, but I could afford it. He answered almost immediately and I figured, from the tone of his voice, that he had been expecting the guy I'd just killed to ring back.

'Madison?'

'Yeah?' He sounded surprised. 'Who's that?'

'Mike Torlin,' I said. 'I thought I'd just ring you to let you know that one of your boys is out here waiting for the cops to turn up with the meat wagon.'

'I don't know what you're talking about, Torlin.' A soft voice, but with a cruel, cunning brain behind it, ticking over like clockwork, wondering why things had gone wrong, determined to give nothing away.

'That's funny, Madison,' I said. 'He tried to kill me at Donati's carnival. Used a gun with a silencer, only he wasn't quick enough.'

There was silence for a moment. I could hear the line humming faintly.

'You still there, Madison?' I asked finally.

'Yeah, I'm here, shamus.'

'I just want to warn you that the next time anybody tries to kill me, I'll come gunning for you, Moose.'

'That won't be easy,' he said mildly. 'The boys will be pretty sore about this.'

'You can tell them from me,' I went on without heat, 'that if I see any of them again on the streets, hiding like the rats they are in alleyways, or wherever they are, I'll let them have a magazineful of slugs in their bellies. Get that, Madison?'

'You're talking like a fool, Torlin,' he said softly. There was real menace in his voice now. 'Maybe you're a little smarter than I had you figured for, but not much. Don't try anything stupid, or you'll regret it.'

'Don't be too sure on that point,' I said, and hung up before he could say anything more. That last act was like spitting in his face in full view of his boys. He'd never let me stay alive now, but I hoped I'd riled him so much that he'd make the mistake I was waiting for.

164

As I stepped out of the booth, I looked at my watch. It was almost noon. Somewhere in the distance I heard the far-away wail of a police siren and decided to make myself scarce, in case they started asking any stupid questions. Hammond knew where to find me if he wanted me, and I guessed it wouldn't be long before I had a personal call from him. Meanwhile, I decided to get in touch with Sally Benton.

I jumped a cab and the squad of police cars arrived at the end of the street as we drove off. Out of the corner of my eye I saw them converging on the entrance to the amusement park — uniformed figures piling from them and heading for the carnival. My entire body felt battered and sore as though I had been beaten up systematically. All I wanted to do was to close my eyes and sleep for a whole week, but there were plenty of things to be done before that and I was too keyed up even to keep my eyes shut.

'Where to?' the driver asked as we slipped into the stream of traffic.

I gave him the address of Sally Benton's apartment.

'OK, bud,' the driver said. He let in the clutch and we picked up speed. I leaned back and the people and events of the past few days drifted past my subconscious mind like a ghostly parade, like a film in jerky slow-motion. I found it impossible to shut them out completely.

Helen Crossman, lying with a couple of slugs in her body, dressed as a gruesome bride on a bed of scarlet silk. Was that somebody's idea of a diabolical joke? It certainly seemed it to me.

Then came Claire Morgan, once described as a truly great actress by the New York critics. A woman who hated Johnny Leinster with such a fanatical hatred that she seemed to have been prepared to ruin his entire show to get even with him for something he'd done in the past. She was the one I couldn't quite figure out properly. There had been something odd about the way she'd died. I found myself wondering why that props man back at the theatre hadn't wanted to talk. It was possible that the murderer was somebody known to him and he was scared for his life. I knew a little about the underworld of Chicago. Maybe it was more widespread and more powerful than that in places like New York or Los Angeles. Here, it had been fed and nurtured by guys like Capone and the other great hoodlums of the twenties.

The ghostly parade ended as the cab slid to a halt beside the kerb and the driver said hoarsely, 'This is it, bud. Do you want me to wait?'

I got out and shook my head. 'Never mind,' I said. 'There's no telling how long this will take.' I handed him a five-dollar bill and he took it with the grateful look of a faithful spaniel in his eyes.

Sally Benton's apartment was on the fifth floor of a block of flats. I knocked on the door. Nobody answered and I knocked again, louder this time. There was a sick feeling in the pit of my stomach that I couldn't quite identify. After a few moments, I tried the door. It wasn't locked properly and I decided she couldn't be very far away. When there was no answer to my third knock, I pushed open the door and went inside.

The room was tastefully, though plainly, furnished with a brightly polished table in the middle of the room and a bowl of flowers in the centre. I shouted, 'Sally!' Somewhere in one of the other rooms, I heard a clock ticking insistently, but there was no other answer to my call.

Going into the other room, I found that it was empty also. That left only two more rooms to the apartment. I opened the third door and found myself in the kitchen. There was a pot of coffee on the stove and a cup on the small table. I closed the palm of my hand around the cup. It was still warm, so she hadn't been gone long. I called her name again, then went through into the bedroom. Sally wasn't there either, but there was a sheet of white notepaper pinned to the pillow on the bed. It stood out against the brilliant splash of colour of the eiderdown and I guessed it had been put there deliberately for anybody entering the room to see. Snatching it up, I carried it across to the window and read it.

★ ★ ★

Torlin:

In case you decided to come here for your girlfriend, it's only fair to tell you that unless you cooperate with us, you'll never see her again. Not alive, that is.

Thanks for ringing me about Clance — he always was a poor shot and the cost of living has taken a distinctly downward curve. Don't go to Hammond about this, if you know what's good for your girlfriend.

★ ★ ★

I screwed it up savagely in my fist, then thrust it into my pocket. I noticed that the note had not been signed and it had been typed on cheap notepaper, the kind that could be bought in a host of stores. But I didn't need any signature to tell me who'd written it. I thought that any half-witted moron could have

169

figured out that Moose Madison wouldn't hang around waiting for things to happen once I'd phoned him and he knew his second line of play had failed.

Any moron except for one obvious exception — Mike Torlin!

14

On the Roller Coaster

I went outside fast and stood on the sidewalk, looking around. A tired-looking guy stood lounging against the wall with a half-smoked cigarette hanging from his lower lip. I went over to him.

'Pardon me,' I said loudly, 'but could you tell me where I can locate Miss Benton? Sally Benton?'

He opened one eye lazily and stared at me as though I were asking him how to get to the moon. Then he hitched his body away from the wall and stood swaying slightly. I realized he was already slightly high. 'She's on the fifth floor,' he said, haltingly. 'But you're out of luck, bud. She's already got a guy. Some fella called for her ten minutes ago. You're too late.' His voice relapsed into a droning mumble.

I took out a five-spot and flashed it in

front of his eyes. 'Any idea where they went or what this guy looked like?' I asked.

He seemed to straighten himself up at the sight of the five dollars and reached out with his fingers, clawing the air greedily. There was a mean look in his half-open eyes. 'I ain't seen the guy before,' he mumbled thickly. His breath stank of strong spirits. 'But they had a big black convertible.'

'What did the guy look like?' I persisted. There was nobody else in sight I could ask, so I seemed stuck with the drunk. Even if he told me, I couldn't place much reliance on his description.

'Sure, sure. I got a good look at him. About five-ten or eleven. Broad shoulders with red hair. He seemed in one hell of a hurry.'

'Which way did they go?' That was my last question. I guessed I wouldn't get much more out of him.

'Towards the outskirts.' He pointed shakily, then snatched up the five dollars and stuffed it into the pocket of his jacket.

So that was that. Chicago was a big

place when it came to figuring where Moose Madison would hide one woman. I didn't want to get in touch with Hammond right now, because unless I was very much mistaken he'd pull me in for questioning in connection with the dead hoodlum in the amusement park, and that was the last thing I wanted. So many things were happening outside that it would have been a waste of time to sit inside the Homicide Bureau answering his awkward questions.

I thought about my licence, then thought about Sally Benton and said, 'To hell with the licence.' I walked a couple of blocks to the nearest bar, went inside and ordered a double Scotch. There was the feeling of inexorable time urging me to a decision, but I couldn't think straight at the moment, and it was essential that I didn't go blundering into anything with my eyes shut, as Moose Madison would be expecting me to do. When I'd phoned him about the death of his hireling, I'd expected to push him into something rash. Then I'd step in and pin him. But something had backfired in my face.

Now, I was the one who was being pushed into hasty actions.

I had a couple of drinks to steady my mind and tried to think things out clearly. I couldn't go to Hammond. I couldn't barge in on Madison and expect him to be there, at the ranch house. By now, he would have skipped the joint and taken up residence somewhere else. Only if I could locate that 'somewhere else', would I find Sally Benton.

Thinking like that was beginning to give me a headache. I tried to put myself in Madison's shoes and thought about all of the various possibilities over another drink, and it was then that I had a flash of inspiration. If I couldn't go to see Hammond — and everything seemed to be lined up against such an interview — there was one other person in Chicago who might be able to help me.

Johnny Leinster.

It wasn't going to be easy; in fact, it was going to be tricky. I guessed Hammond would still have him locked away in the cells at the Homicide Bureau, and that meant I'd have to enter the lion's den if I wanted to see my man. There were two points against that. Firstly, Hammond might be there, or have left word for me to be arrested on sight; and secondly, Madison or one of his men might be already on my tail, watching my every move and phoning them back to Moose. If they saw me going into the Homicide Bureau, nothing would convince them that I'd gone to see Leinster and not Hammond.

I left the bar and hailed another cab. It was a little more than ten blocks to the Homicide Bureau. I got out of the cab two blocks from the Bureau and started to walk the rest of the way. Twice I stopped and looked quickly behind me, but there was nobody on my tail. Maybe I'd been lucky and thrown them off the scent. Maybe, with Sally Benton in their hands, they had decided it wasn't necessary to keep track of my movements. They would just have to call me and threaten to kill her to get me to come running.

I began to get that lonely and helpless feeling. Twenty yards from the Homicide

Bureau, I stood in a shop doorway and waited for a little while. There was no unusual activity around the place, so I guessed Hammond was either away or lurking around in his office. Finally, I plucked up courage and went inside. The desk sergeant looked up and eyed me curiously. I thought I detected an expression of amazement on his features, but it was gone almost instantly, and I couldn't be completely sure.

'I'd like to have a word with my client,' I said, trying to sound more confident than I felt.

'Donati?'

'That's right.'

The desk sergeant looked dubious. 'Well — ' he rubbed his chin thoughtfully. 'I'm not sure. The lieutenant's out on a case at the moment and it isn't usual to — '

'That's OK,' I said hurriedly. 'Hammond knows about this. I thought he'd left word before he went.'

The other shook his head ponderously, then brightened as the meaning behind my words penetrated. 'Sure, Mr. Torlin. If it's OK by the lieutenant I guess it'll be all right.' He climbed down from behind the desk, took a bunch of keys from a rack behind him and led the way into the corridor, past Hammond's glass-panelled door which was tightly closed, and through into the cells.

'A visitor to see you, Mr. Donati,' he called, and I saw Leinster uncurl himself from the cot in the cell and stand up, yawning. I went inside and the Sergeant locked the door behind me.

'How are you getting along, Mike?' He shook me by the hand, then waved me to the cot. I sat down on the edge. 'What can I do for you? Has anything turned up yet?' There was a pleading note in his voice that hadn't been there when I'd visited him before.

'Plenty's turned up,' I said hurriedly, 'but I'm afraid there isn't time to give you all the details. I want to be away from here before Hammond turns up. He's likely to hold me for questioning and something's due to break any minute.'

'Sure, sure, I understand.' Leinster spoke softly, licking his lips. 'What can I do for you, Mike?'

'I'm hoping you can give me some information, Johnny,' I said.

'I'll do my best. What is it you want to know?'

'One of Madison's men tried to kill me a couple of hours ago in the fairground. I was forced to shoot him.'

'He's dead?' Leinster looked mildly surprised.

'I'm afraid so. A bullet in the side and another through the brain. I reckon that Hammond's out there now, taking a look at the body.'

Leinster grimaced. 'I heard they'd closed the carnival. What were you doing around there?'

I grinned. 'I thought I might be able to pick up a lead. I wanted to take a closer look at that roller coaster. Things are breaking pretty fast with this case, and I wanted to stay one jump ahead of the others, even if it's just for the sake of my skin.'

'Go on,' he murmured.

'I want to ask you about Moose Madison. He's one of the people you know better than most. You probably won't be able to answer all of my questions, but at least I'm hoping you may give me something definite to go on.'

Leinster clasped his hands in front of him, locking them around his knees. He swayed gently backward and forward for a moment before answering. 'All right, Mike. Go ahead and ask your questions.'

'First of all,' I began, 'where do you think Madison would head for if he wanted to hide from the police?'

'You mean here in Chicago?'

'Yes.'

He pursed his lips in concentration. Then he said, 'Well, he had a ranch house out north, just off the highway.'

I shook my head. 'No use, I know about that place. I don't think he'll be there now.'

Leinster raised his eyebrows. 'You've been there?'

'That's right. A couple of days ago. I thought Hammond would have told you.'

'No, he certainly didn't mention it. But what's all this leading up to, Mike? Maybe if you let me in on the rest of the deal, I can help still further.'

'OK,' I said. 'I tried to get Madison to make a mistake by hurrying him when I phoned about the death of his boy this morning. Then I went across town to Sally Benton's apartment to see how she was feeling. When I finally got there, I found this note. It was pinned to the pillow in the bedroom. She hadn't been gone all that long; the coffee in the cup was still warm.'

Leinster took the crumpled note, spread it out flat on his knee, and read it quickly. When he finally looked up, he said, 'I can see why you've come to me, Mike. He means all of this, but I suppose you've guessed that already. He's a killer, especially now you've set yourself up against him. He must figure that you know a lot about him, or he wouldn't go to all this trouble.'

'Do you think I can locate him before he kills her, Johnny?'

'It may be possible.' Leinster nodded his head slowly, thinking. I waited. Then he said, 'We can exhaust his old haunts pretty rapidly. You say he'll no longer be at the ranch house. Then I guess there are only two other places you might be likely to locate him.'

'What are they?' I asked quickly.

'Either he's holed up at McCready's bar near the docks, or he's taken advantage of Hammond's closing order and set himself up in the fairground.'

'Thanks, Johnny,' I said quickly. I got to my feet. 'I'll let you know how things pan out. If everything goes according to plan, you should be out of here in a couple of days.' I shouted for the desk sergeant and waited impatiently while he unlocked the door. There was a phone ringing in the outer office.

As we reached the end of the corridor, a young kid, fresh from pounding the beat, came hurrying forward. 'Phone for you, Sergeant,' he said breathlessly. 'It's the lieutenant. Something urgent, I believe.'

I nodded and made for the door. 'I'll let you know if anything happens, Sergeant,' I said loudly. 'Thanks for letting me see Leinster.'

'Any time.' I saw the sergeant climb up

behind his desk and lift the phone to his ear. The next minute, I was outside and melting into the crowd before he got around to calling me back or sending that fresh young copper after me.

At the corner of the block, I found a phone box and slipped inside. The number of McCready's bar was in the book and I slipped in a nickel and dialled it. There was a pause, then a richly gravelled voice at the other end said, 'McCready's bar. Who's that calling?'

I wrapped my handkerchief over the mouthpiece of the phone and said hoarsely, 'This is Rudy. Is the boss there?'

'Rudy? No, he isn't here. We haven't seen Moose for a couple of weeks. Was he on his way down here?'

This guy was asking too many personal questions, and I didn't like it. 'No. I went out to the ranch house, but he'd gone, so I figured he might be out there. You're sure he hasn't been down?'

'Positive, Rudy. I'll let him know you were asking for him if he shows up.'

'OK,' I said shortly and hung up. That narrowed things down a bit. I thought over what Leinster had said, and the more I thought about it, the more it seemed to make sense. Even Madison would have figured that the last place I'd look for Sally Benton would be the fairground, knowing it to have been closed. It must have surprised him to know that I'd been there that afternoon; but to his way of thinking, I'd played right into his hands. I wasn't likely to go back there again. I thought about it some more and realized there wasn't much I could do until it got dark. There was no sense in wandering around the place in broad daylight; that way, I'd just be making myself a target for a few more trigger-happy gunmen.

I went back to the office and brought out another spare clip of slugs for the Luger. This time, I wasn't going to take any chances. By the time I'd found something to eat, it was nearly nine o'clock. Maybe I was heading out on a wild goose chase, or maybe Leinster had been right in his guess; I couldn't be sure.

Before leaving the office, I switched off the light, went over to the window overlooking the street, twitched aside the curtain and looked out. The street looked deserted, but only on the surface. There were a couple of cars a little way along the street and two guys sitting behind the wheels. They looked innocent enough from a distance, but I wasn't taking any chances. I let myself out of the back way, slipped across a patch of waste land dotted with piles of rubble and loose bricks, and reached a low wooden fence that divided it from the street beyond. There was a light on the other side of the fence. I took an upward jump, caught the top of the fence with my fingers and levered myself up on to my hands. There was a tall guy immediately below me with a soft felt hat pulled down well over his eyes.

So they'd decided to watch the back exit too, just to be on the safe side. I rolled over the top of the fence and landed heavily across the big guy's shoulders. He had half-turned by the time I hit him and there was a sudden, startled expression on the pale blur of his face before I pushed him down into the sidewalk. He tried to buck me off, sliding

184

his feet along the ground, his free hand digging for the bulge under his right arm. Before his fingers could close around the gun, I hit him on the side of the head with the heel of my hand, hard. He uttered a low, moaning cough and slumped forward onto his face. His breath whistled out of his lungs in a thin, bleating gasp. The gun slipped from the holster and clattered on to the sidewalk.

I hit him again behind the ear as his fingers scrabbled for the gun; then I kicked it out of his reach, got up slowly and ground my heel down onto his outstretched hand. He uttered a low, gasping scream as I put my weight on my heel, and tried to squirm away, but I kicked him hard in the small of the back. While he threshed on the sidewalk, moaning softly, I picked up the gun and slipped it into my pocket.

'Maybe you'll learn not to try anything like that again, punk,' I said harshly.

He didn't answer and I left him stretched out on the sidewalk, his face buried in his elbows, his legs flung out against the low fence.

My watch said nine fifty as I approached the entrance to the deserted fairground. The looming bulk of the roller coaster stood out against the darkness of the sky. I wondered whether Madison and his bunch of hired killers were in the grounds already; and if so, where they were and what they were doing.

It looked a nice quiet place for somebody to die. There was a stretch of damp grass that separated the street from the amusement park and I made my way slowly across it, instead of going in by the main entrance as they were probably expecting me to do. I figured they couldn't have enough men to patrol the whole perimeter of the park, so I stood a good chance of slipping through without being seen. The dark shapes of the sideshows rose square and massive on either side of me as I slipped in among them.

So far, I'd seen nobody. The whole place was as silent as a tomb. At that moment, I'd have welcomed the sound of a human voice, even the small pop of a

186

silenced pistol. It would have been something tangible, something on which I could focus my spinning brain.

I turned into a wider lane that ran alongside the Hall of Fun. Usually the lights were splashed in a glittering array of colour across the entrance, but now it was dark and seemingly lifeless. At the end of the lane I turned the corner — and almost before I knew what was happening, something chopped down at me from the shadows. My reflexes must have been pretty slow, because the blow took me on the shoulder before I could jump back out of the way.

The tall, thin-faced guy lunged forward to follow up his advantage and I heard him grunt as my bunched fist took him in the stomach, driving him backwards against the wall. There was a faint flash of light on something in his hand and I caught him in a simple judo lock, twisting his arm up and around his back. His head went down as I slipped my other arm beneath his and around the back of his neck.

I guessed he'd try to open his mouth

and shout the moment I released the hold, and that made me more nervous than usual. Otherwise, I would have thought twice about mussing up one of Moose Madison's hoodlums. Releasing my hold on him smartly, I kicked upwards with my knee, hurling him backwards. He wasn't all that heavy and I heard his body strike the wall behind him with a dull thud.

When he didn't move or utter a further sound, I bent and examined him. His neck was broken. I got up again and went forward into the darkness. At least I knew where I stood. Madison was here all right, and he'd got his men placed out at intervals, ready to jump me the moment I showed my face.

The sound of low voices stopped me in my tracks. I edged my way slowly forward again, placing my feet carefully. Madison's voice reached me from the blackness. He was speaking softly. 'You're wrong if you think this guy Torlin will break in and get you out of here. I've got my men ready to grab him if he puts his nose into the fairground tonight.'

'Are you crazy?' Sally Benton's voice. I could detect a faint quiver in it.

'Not really. Just cautious.'

I took a brief look round the corner. By now my eyes had grown used to the darkness and I could just make out the two figures standing immediately inside the booth. One was Madison, the other Sally Benton. I couldn't see anybody else. Somebody moved at the far end of the lane, then walked away into the distance, and I decided to ignore that danger. I walked forward quickly, jumping the last couple of feet. Madison half-turned, bringing up the gun as he saw who it was.

There was a silencer on his gun, none on mine. I didn't want to press that trigger if I could help it. The sound of a shot would bring all the other hoodlums popping out of the sideshows; and even if I managed to kill Madison, they would be able to pour a hail of slugs into Sally and myself before we'd gone fifty yards. My only chance was to silence him without any noise. He twisted violently in my grasp and swung up his arm. The gun moved inexorably downwards until it was pointed a little way above my head.

'So you managed to slip through my men, Torlin?' Madison gasped the words out harshly.

'That's right,' I muttered through my teeth. 'You're finished, Madison. Get that?'

He laughed deep down in his throat and pressed the gun closer towards my head. Desperately, I hurled him away from me and dived for his knees. He wasn't expecting such a manoeuvre and toppled over backwards, squirming beneath me as we hit the ground. There wasn't much time to waste, so I bunched my fist and hit him full in the face. His teeth bit into my knuckles and I felt the skin split across the bone. The pain of the blow jarred along my forearm and I almost cried out with the searing agony.

Madison's head jerked back on his neck and he uttered a low, bleating cough before slumping to the ground. I got up, breathing heavily, and looked down at him. There was a thin pencil of blood oozing from the corner of his mouth.

He was still breathing, but I figured he

wouldn't come round for an hour or so. I went over to Sally Benton and found her arms tied securely behind her back. There was another thin cord wound tightly around her ankles. Swiftly, I cut her free and helped her to her feet. 'You all right, Sally?' I asked hurriedly.

'Yes, I think so. How did you manage to find me?'

'No time to answer that, Sally,' I muttered. 'We've got to lose these hoodlums. The way they must be feeling right now, they'll put a slug into us the minute they spot us.'

She rubbed her ankles where the cord had bit deep into the flesh. She swayed slightly as I held her upright. 'Feeling OK now?' I asked her.

She nodded. We moved away into the darkness, leaving the unconscious body of Moose Madison on the ground beside the sideshow. Sooner or later, one of his hirelings would find him, and then the chase would be on.

We were halfway to the entrance when a shout from behind warned me that we had been seen. I grabbed hold of Sally's arm again and pulled her along. 'For Pete's sake, run!' I hissed.

There was a pop from behind us, and a slug whined over our heads and went singing into the night. Sally started to run, stumbling a little. I had the Luger in my free hand, but I couldn't turn and use it because of Sally's dead weight on my other arm.

A dark figure moved across my line of vision. There was another guy behind him. They started running towards us, blocking our way of escape. I looked around me, wildly. I didn't mind shooting it out with them myself; but with Sally around, things were different. We reached the entrance to the roller coaster and they were closing in on us, fast. I tugged at Sally's hand. 'Come on,' I muttered urgently, 'there's our only chance.'

She halted in her tracks and looked up, scared. 'Up there? But we'd be done if they got us up there, Mike.'

'It's our only hope.'

We went up the low rise and stepped into one of the cars. Savagely, I released the brake and we started forward, gathering speed. Soon, everything became a sweeping blur as the cars rose and dipped, carrying us with them. I hung on to the iron rail at the front of the car and threw a swift glance behind us. There was nothing there but darkness.

We plunged down into a pit of stygian blackness and Sally screamed thinly. Then my stomach hit my ribs as we swung up again. The next time round, I saw two of the hoodlums standing beside the rail. They were steadying their guns on us as we swung towards them. Reaching out, I grabbed Sally by the arm and dragged her down. 'Keep your head down, Sally,' I yelled, but my voice was lost in the grinding din of the car on the rails. 'They're going to shoot.'

Heads low, we rattled towards the waiting gunmen. I could just see the flashes of their guns, then the hiss of slugs striking the metal sides of the car. A split second later we were past them and dropping downwards.

'You all right, Sally?'

She lifted her head. 'Yes, I'm OK.'

We plunged again into darkness. The roar of the metal runners of the cars hammering and grinding on the rails thundered in my ears. Was Madison still unconscious? Or was he hurrying there to pick me off himself? The car slowed as we approached the top of the next bump. I held my breath and looked out for the gunmen. When we dipped down again, I couldn't see them, and guessed they were waiting in the shadows for us. Then I threw a quick glance over the side of the car and saw the place below swarming with other guys.

Cops!

So Hammond hadn't waited for me to turn up at his office. Maybe he'd even had a few quiet words with Johnny Leinster. I started to breathe more easily again. When we came to a halt at the end of the roller coaster, Hammond was there waiting for us.

'So you thought you could double-cross me, Torlin,' he said abruptly. 'I warned you what would happen if you did that again. There are enough charges against you to put you inside for good.'

'For killing a couple of hoodlums,' I said evenly.

'That's right. A couple of hoodlums.' He glared at me. 'Still, I suppose you did hand over Moose Madison to us. We've got to be thankful for that.'

I pulled out a packet of cigarettes, offered one to Sally, then took one myself. My heart was still thumping madly against my ribs. Out of the corner of my eyes, I saw a handful of men being led away. Moose Madison was a limp figure hanging between a couple of uniformed men.

15

The End of the Line

Back at the Homicide Bureau, Hammond said venomously, 'I suppose you had it all figured out from the very beginning, Torlin.'

I shook my head. 'Not really,' I said. 'But you might as well hear the whole of it, now that my client has been released.'

Hammond shrugged his shoulders. 'So?'

'The props man at the theatre where Claire Morgan died gave me the first clues. He refused to talk to me about who had handled the gun which killed her. I guessed from that, that he knew what had happened. There were only two reasons why he wouldn't talk — unless he'd killed her himself, and I didn't believe that. Either the killer was somebody so big and important that even with police protection, they would kill him for squealing, or — '

'Or what?' interrupted Leinster.

'Or he knew that Claire Morgan had put that bullet in the murder weapon herself.'

There was a stunned silence at that. Hammond looked at me as though I were insane. Sally Benton looked slightly shocked. Only Leinster appeared to be unmoved, as if expecting it.

'You're lying,' said Hammond softly.

I shook my head. 'No, Lieutenant. But I'll admit I didn't believe it possible myself until I went to see Claire Morgan's doctor. He told me that she was suffering from some incurable blood disease. She had only a month or so to live even if she was lucky. So I figured that this was the clue I needed. Claire Morgan hated Johnny Leinster more than anything else in the world. Even more than her own life. She did her best to ruin his business after he'd turned her down twenty years ago. She'd never forgiven him for that. But in the end, I think she realized that mere blackmail wasn't hurting him enough, and even the idea of wrecking the carnival finally lost its appeal. So she decided to kill him, but very subtly. She was an actress — a damned good one, at that — and I think the idea of dying as she had been told she would, didn't appeal to her. So she decided to take the easy way out: suicide. Only, it was to look like murder, and Leinster was to get the rap.'

Hammond sat up at that. 'Can you prove any of this, Torlin?' he asked harshly.

'So far, it's all been mere supposition. But I think the props man will talk now if you ask him. It isn't a secret any longer about Claire Morgan. The legend she's built up around herself has fallen in ruins. Yes, I think you'll find he'll talk.'

'OK, I will take your word for it.' Hammond nodded. 'But where does Madison fit into the picture?'

'He came in with Claire Morgan. When Johnny Leinster backed out of the rackets twenty-five years ago, Madison stayed behind and took the rap when the big clean-up came. He also wanted to get even with Johnny. He didn't know much about Claire Morgan at the beginning, but when things started heating up he decided to get into the act. He'd kept in touch with things all the time he'd been in San Quentin.'

'And who tried to brain you from the roller coaster?' Hammond wanted to know.

'That was Claire Morgan. She couldn't wait to get even with Johnny. When she saw me come from the tent she mistook me for him. We're about the same build and in the darkness she couldn't be sure. The attempt failed, but she thought I'd recognize her. So she made a second attempt. She tried to ram my car as I was leaving my office to come down here.'

'OK, Mike, I'll take your word for it.' Hammond got up and stood glaring down at me. 'Is that all?'

'I think so,' I said.

'All right. Then you can go. But for Pete's sake, don't get into my hair again. Since I've been on this case, I've been closer to heart failure than ever before. Now get out before I put you into the cells with Madison.'

'I'm going, Charles,' I said sweetly. I made the door before he exploded.

Outside, Johnny Leinster said, 'I knew I was doing the right thing when I hired you, Mike.'

'Thanks,' I said. 'I'll be seeing you.' I watched him walk away, then moved towards the corner where Sally Benton stood waiting.

THE END

We do hope that you have enjoyed reading this large print book.

Did you know that all of our titles are available for purchase?

We publish a wide range of high quality large print books including:
Romances, Mysteries, Classics
General Fiction
Non Fiction and Westerns

Special interest titles available in large print are:
The Little Oxford Dictionary
Music Book, Song Book
Hymn Book, Service Book

Also available from us courtesy of Oxford University Press:
Young Readers' Dictionary
(large print edition)
Young Readers' Thesaurus
(large print edition)

For further information or a free brochure, please contact us at:
Ulverscroft Large Print Books Ltd.,
The Green, Bradgate Road, Anstey,
Leicester, LE7 7FU, England.
Tel: (00 44) **0116 236 4325**
Fax: (00 44) **0116 234 0205**

Other titles in the
Linford Mystery Library:

THE SUBSTANCE OF A SHADE

John Glasby

Soon after moving into Mexton Grange, an old Georgian country house in the Cotswolds, Alice hears disquieting stories and rumours about her new abode: the previous owners had been driven out by a strange, oppressive atmosphere in the house. It was not as if the house was *actually* haunted — rather, it was as if the house was *waiting to be haunted* . . . These five stories of terror and the macabre by John Glasby will tingle the spine on any dark and stormy night.